STRANDED

By

J. E. Timlin

First Published in 2019 by Blossom Spring Publishing

Stranded © 2019 J.E. Timlin

ISBN 978-1-9161735-3-8

E: admin@blossomspringpublishing.com

W: www.blossomspringpublishing.com

Chapter 1

Air racing, the fastest, most exhilarating sport on the planet. Only the world's most exceptional pilots are capable of performing the extreme manoeuvres of the ultra-high speed, low altitude course.

Our planes are the quickest, most agile aircraft ever built. More manoeuvrable than fighter jets, they are streamlined to perfection and finely tuned to increase aerodynamic ability and reduce drag. They can ascend three thousand, seven hundred feet in one minute and navigate a low altitude slalom track at over three hundred and fifty kilometres per hour.

Air racing is tough on the mind, body and nerves but I'd had a great run in yesterday's qualifying event and was psyched, totally focused and all in for a win today. I pulled down the visor on my custom-made helmet and wriggled slightly in my G-suit. "Number 89, you are cleared into the track. Smoke on," the Race Director's voice reached me through my headset.

I was off, shooting through the air-filled pylons of the starting gate, wings level, bang on the entry speed target of two hundred knots. Straight into the chicane, knife-edging the turns. Nice - rhythmical and smooth, got that up-motion curve just right so that I didn't lose lift when my wings were vertical and not acting like wings at all. Out of the chicane, I took a huge lungful of air and strained hard, tensing my calves, thighs and stomach to help me cope with the massive G force as I hurtled straight into a vertical turning manoeuvre – rocketing up and over, inverting the plane completely and diving back down. Even with my breathing and straining techniques and special G-Suit - which stopped blood pooling in my legs and kept it pumping into my head - I saw the pinpricks of light that meant I was close to blackout. The human body just isn't built to deal with the 10 gs of force it was being slammed with now.

A split second later though, I was upright again, perfectly online to the next gate. I swooped through, then pulled hard to the penultimate pylons, no wash-off of speed on the corner – good! A bit of g on the final turn and I was speeding for the finish. I checked the clock: sub 54 seconds, a clean, fast run which took me straight to the top of the leader board. I raised my arm and pumped the air.

"You pretending to air race again?" My best friend Luke leaned into the door-less cockpit of the partially complete kit plane I'd spent the last three years helping his dad, Jim Carter, to build. "You're one sad dude," he shook his head. "You need to come through to the kitchen Captain Nerdy Boy, Mum's made some sandwiches for lunch." He had lifted the earpiece of my headset to talk to me, now he dropped it so that it slapped back hard against my head. "Ow," I grumbled, rubbing my smarting ear.

"Ow," I yelped again as Luke's toddler, sister Alice, known to all as Minx, elbowed past her brother, hauled herself into the cockpit beside me and dragged the earphones off my head. She squashed them onto her own and turned to me, one side was more like an eye-patch than an earphone. "Go Bain, Capn," she demanded, hauling at her harness with her pudgy little hands.

"Not today Minx," I replied. "We'll fly to Spain tomorrow, got to get something to eat now." I scooped

3

her up and climbed out of the plane onto the garage floor. Dangling her by the straps of her dungarees, I trailed Luke out of their large garage, pausing to survey mine and Jim's handiwork with pride.

Three years it had taken Jim and I to get to this point. We'd broken the project down into small pieces, if we hadn't, we'd have been so blown away by the size of the undertaking we'd have given up almost before we started. A Boeing 747 has six million parts. Our little plane wasn't quite that complex but still… Jim and I had become skilled woodworkers and metal workers. We'd taught ourselves to weld, to rivet, even to sew and now, here we were. I beamed from ear to ear, proud creators of a fabulous, almost complete self-build airplane.

I'd learned so much during the build process and topped up my knowledge by trawling aviation manuals and quizzing Jim. I'd practiced incessantly on the fabulous Microsoft Flight Simulator my dad had bought me for my last birthday, perfecting my flying technique. I was sure, given half a chance, I could fly our little plane for real. One day! Sighing wistfully, I headed for the kitchen.

Luke and I ate our ham salad sandwiches whilst Minx tore hers into pieces and dropped them on the kitchen floor. "Dad phoned from Vancouver whilst you were winning races from the garage floor," said Luke between mouthfuls. "He'd just met up with an old school friend who emigrated to Canada a few years ago. The friend and his wife are film makers, which is really cool. In March they're in the Yukon - which is like this big snowy wilderness on the Alaskan border - for a month making a documentary on the impact of oil drilling on the indigenous people – not entirely sure what that means!"

Minx knocked over her juice, Luke shuffled his chair away from the sticky purple liquid dripping from the table and continued talking.

"Anyway, this friend's invited Dad and I, well and Mum and Minx too but Mum says Minx is too small so they're not going, to join him there over the Easter holiday. It'll be partly educational, but Dad's friend says there's some great skiing and snowboarding too." Minx was now mashing her sandwich into the spilled juice.

"He wants us to collect his children in Vancouver, then fly to a place called Whitehorse. From there he's going to charter a small plane, umm …it's name's like some kind of little furry animal…?"

"Beaver," I suggested. Luke frowned, considering, then shook his head. "Otter?"

"That's the one. An otter, for dad to fly to… somewhere in the Yukon, can't remember its name. Dad says you can come too, if you want to?"

'Wow. Did I want to? Did I ever!'– watching a documentary being made and skiing both sounded fantastic, but it wasn't the activities at the destination that I wanted to do most. It was the thought of the journey to the Yukon that excited me – the opportunity to fly, not just in a passenger jet but in a small plane too.

Flying had fascinated me since I was little – I mean, a great metal cylinder, filled with people, hurtling through the air, it's something of a miracle, right? Almost pure magic!! Yet I'd never done it. My dull as dishwater stepdad, Colin was scared to fly and anyhow, he and Mum favoured walking holidays and were of the unwavering belief that there were so many glorious places to hike in the UK that there was no point in going abroad. Whilst other kids packed flip flops and beach towels and headed to the airport every summer, I sullenly chucked walking boots and well used waterproofs in the boot and slumped in the back seat of the car.

Flying was, in fact, what had brought Luke and I together. I'd never had a proper friend before - too shy and well… yeah, if I'm forced to admit it, probably too odd - but one day, six years ago, a new boy had walked into the school yard with his dad. His dad wasn't wearing his jacket or cap, just a white shirt and blue trousers but I'd spotted the epaulets on his shoulders and known he was a pilot right away. "So," I'd overheard him say to Luke, "I'm off to Sydney and the time difference might make it a bit difficult to speak to you over the next couple of days but you'll be fine, I know you'll make a friend right away. Enjoy your first day at your new school."

'That friend's going to be me,' I'd vowed to

myself, my voice booming with determination in my head. Squashing down my usual shyness I had barrelled right up to Luke as his dad walked away and bombarded him with questions right there and then, before the morning bell even rang:

"Your dad's a pilot, isn't he?" I'd gushed. "That's super cool. I've always wanted to know, does a pilot need a key to start the plane's engine? What speed does a plane get up to on the runway before it takes off? How does it even take off, I mean how can something so big and so heavy get off the ground? Does your dad chat to other pilots as they fly, what do they talk about? And what's that white trail a plane leaves behind it in the air?"

Luke had fake staggered backwards, as if the force of my questions was knocking him over and laughed. "Whoa dude, slow down! I don't know the answers to any of those questions, other than 'is your dad a pilot?' To which the answer is yes. I mean, do you know everything about your dad's job? What's your name anyway? I'm Luke."

"Nathan Ellis, Nate," I'd answered, deflated.

"Stepdad, he's a car mechanic – which is like, whoppingly boring! - why would I want to know anything about that?"

But that was how Luke felt too. Despite his dad having the coolest job in the world, Luke had no interest whatsoever in what he did. The two of us were and continue to be, bemused by the other's interest/lack of interest in flying. In fact, we are polar opposites in every way but despite, or perhaps because of our differences (opposites attract and all that) we became firm friends. I insisted that Luke sit beside me in class and the teacher - perhaps mindful of the fact that it would save him having to write 'Nate is a bit of a loner,' in my report again that year - rearranged the seating so it could happen.

His constant shadow, I was referred to by all the other kids as 'Luke's friend Nate.' It soon became the way I'd introduce myself. It never occurred to me to insist I was a person in my own right.

I know it confused and irritated Luke that my interest in flying could not be dented but, though he grumbled, he understood that this was the compromise he had to make. To keep his devoted side-kick he had to give on this one thing. I'd dedicate some of my time to helping his dad, reading aviation manuals and playing on my simulator, otherwise I was all his, I'd follow him anywhere. Well, almost anywhere, I'd had several invites to go on holiday with Luke and his family in the past but Mum and Colin had always said no – I was too young. I was thirteen now though and determined - this time I was going, there was nothing they could do to stop me.

Chapter 2

"Oh, but you'll miss climbing Helvelyn," said Mum when I'd asked permission, pausing after delivering that sentence as though I might actually cry, 'oh, well in that case I'll ditch Luke, forget flying, forego Canada and come with you and Colin to the Lake District for Easter!' I raised my eyebrows but didn't bother to reply, her argument didn't deserve a response.

My step-dad was even less encouraging. "Canada's a long way to go," he said. "And flying," he shuddered, "there's nothing normal about eating your lunch from a tray and watching a movie whilst hurtling at over five hundred miles an hour through the air in a big metal tube! A small plane's even worse, sitting in those big things is bad enough but at least in them you can pretend you aren't really in the air. We've booked a lovely little B and B in the Lake District and Helvelyn is quite challenging at this time of year. Come with us, you'll have fun and we'll know you're safe."

"Flying," I growled, "is the safest form of travel

there is. Only one in eleven million people die in plane crashes. ONE…IN…ELEVEN…MILLION!! One in thirteen thousand are hit by lightning but you don't make me hide under the bed every time there is a thunderstorm! More people are killed by donkeys each year than in planes Colin. Oh, come on, I'm thirteen and I've never been on a plane, it's just not fair."

"Actually," Colin infuriated me by countering, "only five percent of the world's population has ever been on a plane."

'Grr,' I'd given him that fact, I hadn't expected him to use it against me! "Yeess! but that's because most of the world's population lives in developing countries. I don't, I live in England but I don't want to spend my whole life in it, I want to travel. When will I be old enough to get on a plane, sixteen, eighteen, twenty-one? Am I going to have to say on my CV that I spent my gap year building wells in deepest, darkest Northumberland?!" Mum and Colin raised their eyebrows but said nothing. "Dad'll let me go," I said at last, playing my trump card and stomping off up the stairs. "I'm going to call him now."

In my bedroom, I spoke to Dad's answerphone. I can't actually remember the last time I spoke to Dad, but hey, he's a busy man, works hard. 'But manages to spend plenty of time with his new family,' the niggly voice at the back of my head chimed in. I quickly shut it off, I loved my dad, after all, he'd bought me the awesome Microsoft Flight Simulator for my last birthday. 'Though it did arrive two weeks late, probably after Mum called him up and said you've forgotten our son's birthday again,' that petulant voice muttered.

My dad had been gone seven and a half years but I missed him still. He was everything Colin wasn't – impulsive and fun, larger than life - on reflection, a grown-up version of Luke. As far as I was concerned, boring, steadfast Colin could never hope to match up. I really couldn't understand what Mum saw in him.

Dad didn't bother to ring back – busy, busy, busy! But a couple of hours later I got a three-word message – 'go for it.'

I stomped downstairs, "Dad says I can go," I challenged. Mum and Colin were in the kitchen, chopping vegetables side by side, preparing a 'healthy meal' for dinner.

They looked at each other and Colin gave a small, resigned nod, surprising me, I was all geared up for full scale battle. "Okay," Mum sighed, "if you're sure it's what you want to do, I'll speak to Luke's dad, but you need to help Colin in the garage every weekend between now and the holiday to earn your spending money."

So, I spent eight long, tedious Saturdays, half-heartedly 'working' alongside my stepdad. Colin desperately tried to teach me about car engines, I resisted learning. The days dragged, Colin was so boring he should have come with a health warning tattooed to his forehead – 'caution, may cause drowsiness!' But eventually, my sentence was over, the Easter Holiday was here. Mum and Colin had dropped me at our local airport but had not come into the terminal, "costs more to park a car at these places than a small plane," Colin had grumbled. I was furious, but I overheard him muttering to Mum as I dragged my suitcase from the boot, "I just can't go in there Val, better to say goodbye out here."

Now, Jim, Luke and I were charging through Heathrow Airport following a delayed connecting flight, leaping protruding luggage like Olympian hurdlers and shoving toddlers and slow-moving oldies out of our way. At last we collapsed sweating and blowing in our wonderful 'posh seats,' (which we could afford because Jim – hurray - got cheap, staff travel tickets).

Luke had begun to trawl the in-flight entertainment guide as soon as we sat down whilst trying out the different massage options on his seat, "this one gives a butt massage," he giggled, vibrating merrily beside me. "Try it Nate."

I grinned at him, "in a minute." I still needed to quiz Jim on the preparations the pilots would be making up on the flight deck.

"And I always thought it was just like driving a car: you get in, switch on and go," Luke butted in, after Jim had spent about fifteen minutes talking me through all the checklists the pilots would be running through up on the flight deck, the systems they'd be setting up, the checks they'd be performing. I was surprised he'd been listening, he even looked mildly interested and impressed.

"Ah, you see," Jim replied, "I do work for a living."

"Yeah," dismissed Luke, "for at least an hour at the start of each flight."

"Uh huh," Jim agreed sheepishly. "Then we get on with the important tasks of checking out the menu and deciding which films to watch on our laptops."

"Do you do nothing then for the rest of the route?" enquired the leisure-time loving Luke, apparently experiencing his first flicker of interest in following in his dad's footsteps.

"Umm, not nothing, but it's far from hectic. We go into routine monitoring mode - from time to time the pilot not flying - the Pilot Monitoring, will check the instruments. Fuel monitoring's done with the most regularity, usually every thirty minutes - the fuel used will be compared with the expected quantity to make sure all is okay. We'll also listen to and respond to Air Traffic Control. But really, we only begin to work again in earnest an hour before landing, with only the last thirty minutes being fully 'nose to the grindstone.'"

"Hmm," Luke pulled on his earphones, his interest waning as quickly as it had flared. "I'm gonna watch Star Wars followed by The Fast and Furious and I'm gonna order cookies, hot chocolate and chocolate ice-cream on a rotating loop all the way to Canada. Have a good flight guys!"

Five minutes later, before we'd even taken-off he was sound asleep. I looked at him and chuckled. It never seemed to matter where we were or what was going on around us, Luke had the ability of a new born baby to fall asleep, he'd just tilt his head back, close his eyes and check-out totally.

Chapter 3

We spent the first night in a hotel in Vancouver. The next morning, we heard the Fallon children before we saw them. There were four of them and they were clustered around a table in the breakfast room, yakking with a cheery disregard for the other diners around them. As an only child, I was always taken aback by how easily people got along with one another and these children both terrified and fascinated me. It was obvious how fond they were of each other and of their nanny, who handed them over with reluctance, after much hugging and headed off for a fortnight with her own family.

Eight-year-old twins Sasha and Libby were identical to look at but as different as could be in personality terms. Sasha, stuffing bacon into the ever-open mouth of a small brown dog curled on her knee, and eggs and toast into her own, was loud, chatty and majorly inquisitive, a small bundle of manic energy. I stared at her wide-eyed, how was she managing to chew, swallow and burble that cascade of words all at once? Five minutes after meeting her she'd notified us: she was the eldest twin by fifteen minutes and the tallest, asked us three million questions, not really pausing to listen to any answers and; informed us that she hated school, liked the nanny, loved skiing and was excellent at it and had shamed her mum and dad into buying her the dog – Malty. "I told them I missed them too much when they were away filming and needed a friend to keep me company. I tried for a pony," she lamented, "but Dad wouldn't go for it. I've not given up though," she reassured us with a grin, "he'll get sick of me asking and give in eventually." I sincerely believed her.

Towering, sixteen-year-old Harvey, Jim had informed Luke and I back at home, had Asperger Syndrome. The quiet, back country skiing of the Yukon, his dad had told Jim, would be perfect for Harvey who couldn't handle the bustle and noise of a regular ski resort.

Knowing nothing about Asperger's, the three of us had googled the syndrome: 'Difficulty with social interaction, not keen on physical contact and lack of interest in others,' were three common character traits. "Hi, I'm Harvey," the boy greeted us, holding out his huge hand to each of us in turn. "Welcome to Canada, I hope you had a good journey." So much for stereotyping!

He did however, speak in an unnaturally loud voice and talked past, rather than to your face, which was rather unnerving. "Can't do faces," he informed us, clearly used to having to explain himself, "I find them too distracting. People often say one thing whilst their features say another – I can't listen to their words properly whilst I'm trying to work out what their faces are telling me."

Fair enough.

"Dogs have better faces than people," he continued, weaving his fingers into Malty's wiry coat. "They don't do contradictory stuff. When their tails wag their faces are happy, when their ears are down their faces are sad. You always know where you are with a dog. They're far less worrying than people – Malty's always friendly and never ever gets grumpy or angry."

Again, fair enough, couldn't argue with any of that at all.

"I really like planes too," I realised he was addressing me, though it took me a moment to figure out as he was looking over my shoulder, out of the window. "I've flown in an Airbus A320, 330 and 380 and I'd like to fly in a new 350. I've also been in a Boeing 737, 767 and 777 but my favorite is a 787. I've been in a turboprop Dash-8 but I've never flown in a De Havilland Canada DHC-3 Otter."

I was about to reply that I was really looking forward to flying in the Otter too but Harvey continued. "I'm more interested in bodies than planes though, I'm very good at biology and really like medical stuff,"

"Oh, are you going to be a doctor?" I asked. Harvey looked at me, well, to the side of me, as though I were mad.

"No," he gasped, "I love medicine in books but I wouldn't want to deal with a sick or hurt person. No, no, no, no, a real injury!" he gave an exaggerated, comic shudder, "once I'd seen something like that I wouldn't be able to get it out of my mind." Still shaking his head, he stood up from the table abruptly and walked away, interaction over for the time being.

I looked at Luke, his eyes were wide. Ten minutes with Sasha and Harvey and I felt like we'd been hit by a word avalanche. The third sister, Emmeline, thirteen like Luke and I, looked from one to the other of us, her narrowed eyes warning us not to mock or comment on her brother.

In contrast to Harvey, Emmeline looked you directly in the eye, holding your gaze as if she were looking inside your head. She reminded me of a bird, small and slight with dark, watchful eyes. She was definitely not a blurter like her younger sister, you could see she thought about everything she was going to say before she opened her mouth. My initial impression was Emmeline would be uptight, a bit cold but as she shook hands with me, a surprisingly strong hand shake for such a little person, she smiled and it was like the sun had come out. I felt myself grinning stupidly back as I did a complete U-turn on my opinion. There was warmth there, plenty of it. She might have a self-reliant – 'I don't need you, I've got me,' attitude but it didn't mean she was frosty. "Call me Emmie," she said, taking back her hand that I hadn't realised I'd still been holding.

"I'm Luke's friend," I stammered, in time-honoured tradition, "Nate."

"Nate," she said. "Pleased to meet you," and she did, genuinely seem to be. She didn't blank me and fawn over Luke the way other kids did back home, she chatted to me throughout breakfast. I did my best to converse back but was far from skilled – Luke was my only friend and he was so much more interesting than me that I rarely talked, just listened. I wasn't used to chatting with other teenagers, certainly not girl ones!

Chapter 4

After breakfast, we piled into a mini-bus taxi and headed to the airport for a short internal flight to Whitehorse.

En-route, Harvey, so broad he took up all of his own seat and half of the next one, briefed us on our final destination in his loud monotone, whilst staring out of the window.

"The Yukon territory is Canada's last frontier," he lectured, "it is a largely mountainous and forested wilderness in the northwest of the country. We are going to the Vantut National Park. The closest community is Old Crow, population of only three hundred. Imagine," his eyes widened in horror, "living in a town called Old Crow! Whitehorse is a great name, I'd like to live in a place called Whitehorse but Old Crow – that's just a weird, creepy name!" Another of those funny, exaggerated shudders. "Neither the Park nor Old Crow have road access, the closest road is the Dempster Highway, one hundred and nine miles away. At the moment the temperature there is minus eight

Celsius, the all-time low was minus fifty-seven, – now that's really, really cold! Brrr," more comedy shuddering. "The aboriginal people, the Vuntut Gwitchin, that Mum and Dad are filming are dependent on caribou. They have been very active in protesting and lobbying against the possibility of drilling for oil in their territory. I would be too if I were them, I wouldn't want my isolated world invaded by a big bunch of greedy, noisy business people."

As at breakfast, he stopped talking as abruptly as he'd started. He pulled on his noise cancelling ear-defenders and closed his eyes. Sasha took up the monologue, though her subject matter was more wide-ranging and much less relevant. By the time we pulled up outside the airport, we'd learned far more than we needed or wanted to know about her best friend Lisa - who did have a pony and a dog and a hamster; her teacher – Mr. Woodrough, who had sticky out ears and huge crooked teeth but could be quite funny and; her favourite TV programmme – I completely forget, I'd pretty much tuned out by that time!

When we landed in Whitehorse, another taxi

ferried us to the private airstrip. The aviation hangar was a large corrugated, galvanized steel structure with a curved roof. A small plane sat on the tarmac across from the main door, its engine flap – cowling - raised, an engineer busy inside the engine. I felt a buzz of excitement just looking at it.

"Is that ours?" asked Emmi.

"It is," confirmed Harvey. "A De Havilland Canada DHC-3 Otter. A single-engined, high-wing, propeller driven, STOL aircraft."

"STOL - short take off & landing plane," I butted in, Harvey wasn't the only one keen to show off his aviation knowledge. "Perfect for flying around Canada because it can take off and land either on or off airport: on snow or ice with skis; in fields and on gravel riverbanks, using fat, low-pressure tires and; on water, using floats."

"STOL aircraft have large wings for their weight," Harvey wasn't handing over the spotlight without a fight. "As well as coping with a short ground run they have the ability to climb and descend steeply, to quickly clear obstacles like trees."

"Jeez," groaned Luke, "the award for plane nerd of the century goes to.... both of you."

We piled out of the taxi. The girls took Malty off to a patch of rough ground to 'see if he wants to do anything before the flight.' Luke collapsed onto a bench outside the hangar to continue whatever game he was playing on his iPad, oblivious to the cold morning air. Harvey and I trooped after Jim into the terminal, trailing him to the weather office to check the forecast to make sure we could fly.

Weather in Canada in March is not always conducive to flying. A SIGMET – Significant Meteorological Information advisory – warning pilots of severe or hazardous weather conditions had been in place for the previous two days but had been withdrawn yesterday afternoon. Jim wanted to check that it had not been re-issued. There was heavy cloud cover this morning, ice could form on a plane as it flew through cloud. If there was any danger of severe icing Jim would not take the flight. Ice could reduce a small plane's aerodynamic efficiency, weighing it down. In extreme circumstances, it could even cause a crash.

Jim studied the aerodrome forecasts intently, stroking his chin and muttering to himself. "Is everything OK?" I asked, I had my fingers, toes and everything else crossed, I'd be gutted if he decided we couldn't fly.

"Mmmm," Jim replied. "The forecasts aren't ideal, but they rarely are at this time of year, in fact we're lucky to be flying today, the long-range forecast is awful. Today's weather looks as good as it going to get for at least the next week. The conditions are marginal for visual flight but that's not a problem, I'll transfer to instruments if necessary."

What Jim meant was, that if he could no longer see a sufficient distance from the cockpit window, he would switch to navigating solely by reference to the plane's instrument panel. Visual Flight Rules (VFR) is the most common mode of operation for small aircraft but it is only safe to fly VFR when outside references can be clearly seen from a sufficient distance. When flying through clouds or thick falling snow, flight by visual reference is not safe and a pilot must convert to the more complex Instrument Flight Rules. Used to flying big jets, Jim was accustomed to instrument flying, this would not worry him.

"So, we're good to go then?" I asked. 'Please, please say yes.'

"Yep, good to go."

'Yeess!'

"Are you going to file a flight plan?" enquired Harvey

Aha, an opportunity to show off my superior knowledge at last. "No flight plan," I said quickly, before Jim could explain. "We'll be low level flying, our route's too remote to be covered by radar. We don't file a plan, just tell air traffic control where we're taking off, what time we're leaving, where we're flying to and our expected arrival time."

"A Flight Following Service," Harvey nodded. Hmff, he did know about it. "We'll need to make a phone call within one hour of our estimated landing time otherwise ATC will start Lost Aircraft procedures."

"That's right," grinned Jim, looking from one to the other of us, enjoying our game of 'I-know-the-most tennis.' "Right, let's go out to the plane so I can oversee the fueling and see how the engineer is getting on out there."

We walked across the crunchy, frosty tarmac to the little plane. The cowling was still up, the engineer leaning against it, talking into his phone, waving around a wrench - arguing with someone it looked like. As we neared, he ended his call, Jim greeted him and introduced Harvey and I. The man was polite but curt, a little distracted, "almost finished," he said, nodding at the engine.

"Anything wrong," enquired Jim as the engineer's phone began to ring again.

The guy shook his head, "nah, just routine maintenance and an oil change, I've fitted a new oil filter too." He scowled at his ringing phone.

Jim nodded. "On a piston engine such as this, the oil is changed after every twenty-five hours of flying time," he told Harvey and myself.

The engineer pushed the engine flap down, laid down his wrench and excused himself, answering his phone as he walked away, speaking in a low, surly tone.

Jim commenced his walk about, trailed by Harvey and I, performing a visual check of the condition of the aircraft.

The plane was fitted with wheel-skis at both the front and back. It had tyres but small skis were slotted round them, slightly raised above the wheel. "Do you need to raise the wheels to land on the skis?" I asked Jim.

He shook his head, "these ones aren't hydraulic, they're called penetration skis. If the plane comes down on hard ground only the wheels will touch-down but if it lands on a soft surface the wheels will sink in and the skis come into play."

By the time Jim had finished his walk-about, the engineer had returned. Jim told him how much fuel to load, then we collected the others and our vast array of luggage – skis and snowboards as well as suitcases – and boarded the plane.

Harvey, not wanting to be squashed in close proximity to anyone else, grabbed the seat at the back of the plane, just in front of the cargo net where we'd stashed our luggage. Luke flopped into the first seat, eyes glued to iPad and the girls sat together in the middle, Sasha with Malty on her knee, 'so he can look out of the window!'

I squeezed in beside Jim on the spare cockpit seat, watching as he performed his before-start checks and procedures, switching on the battery, instruments, GPS and radio. "So," he held the aviation map so I could see it, "this is the route we'll take if we can," he ran his finger along the map. "Our trip, Whitehorse to Old Crow is four hundred and seventy-three miles but of course we can't fly that far on one load of fuel. We'll head for Dawson City, two hundred and thirteen miles away," he pointed to the airfield, "but if the weather stops us getting in there we'll re-route to Fairbanks, he moved his finger across the map. "Fairbanks is a military airport, but we'll be able to re-fuel there if we have to. I've had the engineer put additional fuel in the reserve tanks just in case we rack up extra miles routeing round bad weather."

I nodded; I'd forgotten that the Otters had additional fuel tanks in the wingtips. Jim was being ultra-cautious, making sure that if the weather forced us to take a much less direct route to Old Crow we could, or that, if we got there but couldn't land we'd have plenty of fuel to get us safely to somewhere else where we could put down.

"As you can see," continued Jim, "we're headed over a lot of high-ground, if the weather worsens we'll re-route down the valleys, get down below the clouds and the worst of the weather in the best way we can."

"Do you want me to get the ATIS?"

Jim nodded. I turned the radio dial to the frequency for the ATIS, the Automatic Terminal Information Service. A recorded voice communicated the airport weather in aviation language. Roughly translated it went something like this: 'Whitehorse ATIS at 0150 hours (in aviation, time is always given in UTC – Coordinated Universal Time - regardless of the country). Runway 32 in use. Wind 330 degrees at 5 knots. Scattered cloud at 7,000 feet, overcast at 14,000 feet, Temperature minus 5 degrees Celsius. Dewpoint minus 8 degrees Celsius. Altimeter 29 point 45 inches.

Jim nodded and set his altimeter subscale to

give the accurate aircraft altitude. He passed me the checklists. Once I'd taken him through them, he pulled on his headset and radioed Ground. I pulled on a spare headset so I could hear their exchange. "Ground, good morning Charlie-Alpha-Delta-X-ray-Hotel, Apron 2 requesting start for northerly departure to Old Crow."

A broad grin spread across my face, all the times I'd played at this, sitting in the kit plane in Jim's garage. Finally, here I was, experiencing it for real. C-ADXH was our plane's registration and therefore also our call-sign, Apron 2 our parking area. I got a real kick out of this pilot speak.

"C-ADXH, departure runway 32 right, maintain runway heading, climb 10,000 feet, squawk 1200," came the reply.

A squawk is a code that is transmitted by the aircraft and picked up by Air Traffic Control radars to identify either a specific aircraft or the type of flight. 1200 is a generic code for visual flight in North America.

Jim responded, as he was expected to each time, relaying back the exact information he'd just been given. "All buckled in?" he asked. I gave him a thumbs-up. "All set down the back?" he called, lifting his headset so he could hear the chorus of positive replies from Luke and the Fallon children. "Good," he nodded then started the huge radial engine – a loud whir at first, the propellers beginning to turn slowly, then a roar as all nine cylinders fired. The propeller was rotating fully now, vibrations were running through the plane, the draft buffeting it slightly. Exhaust plumes wafted past the cockpit window, it was fabulous. Jim gestured to me to take him through the After-Start Check List. "C-ADXH Apron 2 request taxi," he radioed Ground when we'd finished.

"C-ADXH taxi Echo, hold short of 32 left."

Jim replied, released the brake, upped the power and steered the small plane slowly, using the rudder pedals, towards the designated runway. Just before we reached it, Air Traffic Control spoke again. "C-ADXH after the landing regional jet, cross 32 left to holding point 32 right behind."

"Behind the landing Regional Jet, clear to taxi to 32 right, behind," Jim responded.

"There's a jet coming in to land on the longer commercial runway." He took a moment to explain to me, "we're instructed to wait for it to land before crossing its runway to the one we'll depart from."

We watched the jet come in over our heads and vacate the runway, then taxied to our holding point where Jim performed the Before Take Off Check List. Man, they really did like these check lists, but I guess the 'better safe than sorry motto' is never more relevant than when launching yourself ten thousand feet into the air in a metal tube!

"C-ADXH contact tower 118.3," said Ground.

I saw Jim turn the radio dial to call the tower on a new frequency, "Tower, good morning C-ADXH, holding point 32 right ready for departure."

Tower replied, "Wind 330 degrees at 5 knots. Runway 32 right clear take–off."

"Runway 32 clear take off C-ADXH," responded Jim. "Here we go," he grinned at me and we were off, throttling hard, dashing down the runway then leaping off the ground, launching upwards.

The roar of the engine, the throbbing power, the

bone shaking vibration from the propeller and the noisy rush of air down the side of fuselage would have been viewed by some as uncomfortable and unpleasant. Not me, no way, I was so delighted by the experience I actually laughed out loud and clapped my hands like an excited toddler. I was momentarily embarrassed, but I looked at Jim and saw him grinning at me and knew he understood. That even after all the times he'd taken off, he still got a kick out it. That great rush and surge, it was awesome.

"Continue with Edmonton Centre 132.1," signed off Air Traffic Control, "have a safe flight,"

"132 decimal 1, C-ADXH, thanks, g'bye." Jim replied, signing off.

We climbed rapidly, then levelled off as we reached our cruising altitude of ten thousand feet. It would be at least twenty degrees below freezing point outside and we'd climbed through thick cloud into crystal clear, silver blue air. I saw Jim's eyes scanning the window and did the same. I could see a thin, intricate tangle of ice had crept from the bottom corner of the cockpit windshield. Jim noticed it too and flicked a switch.

"The de-icing boots?" I asked. Jim nodded. He'd just inflated the rubber along the wing's edge to crack the ice and make it flake off. It was dangerous to let it build there, it would make the wings heavier, at best slowing us down and throwing out our flight timings and calculations, at worst reducing our lift or possibly freezing our control surfaces – our ailerons and flaps - causing us to crash.

"Just follow me through - put your hands on the control column, feel what I'm doing," Jim said after a while. The Otter had dual control columns; I took lightly hold of the one in front of my seat. Jim pushed forwards and mine shifted, the movement was subtle. "Tiny movements," Jim said. The plane tilted forwards gently and we descended. Jim reversed the manoeuvre, then banked the plane left and right. As soon as he'd put the plane into a turn he brought the control column back the centre. "You don't need to hold the plane in a turn the way you would a car," he explained. "Once you've put on an angle of bank it will stay there, the plane will maintain it."

"Think you can do it yourself?" he asked.

"Me? Fly? Seriously? You bet I can!"

"Okay," Jim lifted his hands from the control column, waggling them dramatically in the air. "You have control."

I flew straight for a short while. Jim had me push the throttle in to speed us up, pull it back to slow our speed, then to ascend and descend slightly. I was too heavy handed to begin with – "you're not air racing now," Jim smiled, "no hauling and pulling, gently does it." Soon, I got a feel for just how subtle my adjustments needed to be. "Righto," Jim said, "let's get you to do some work. We're on a heading of 010 degrees, turn us right onto a heading of 050, you'll need an angle of bank of about 30 degrees."

I nudged the control column to the right to initiate the turn, the airplane immediately started slipping – pivoting on its axis, the tail falling slightly into the turn. I gasped and widened my eyes at Jim, expecting him to grab his controls. He remained calm. "Just put in a bit of right rudder to compensate," he advised. "Okay good, but now you're losing lift in the turn." I nodded, concentrating hard, we were beginning to descend, I pulled back on the control column to lift my nose and the descent arrested. Jim nodded, "fantastic, but now you've pitched up you have drag, put a bit of throttle on."

"Phew," I blew out a breath. "It's not as simple as it looks is it?"

Jim shook his head. "There's a lot that can go wrong in a turn, every action has a knock-on effect, light hands and feet are a must, subtlety is key. Okay, now roll out of that turn, bring your control column to the left, then centralise. Take your feet off the rudders. Let the nose flatten."

"I missed the heading," I moaned miserably.

Jim patted my shoulder, "never expected you not to. Everyone overshoots when they're learning. What you need to do is start rolling out of the turn ten degrees before you hit your heading. You waited until you hit fifty degrees to stop banking, so you turned too far."

He took hold of his control column again. "You have control," I said, handing over. "That was awesome, thanks."

As we flew, I glued my forehead to the side window, craning my neck to watch the changing terrain through the occasional gap in the clouds. Very quickly the landscape became mountainous, craggy white-capped peaks, dense, dark forested areas, frozen snowmelt lakes and glistening white river valleys. It was mind blowing, dramatic, and stunningly beautiful, I was really, really enjoying this flight.

We got down into and refuelled at Dawson City without incident and had been flying for just short of two hours when the weather worsened. One minute the air was sparklingly clear outside my window, giving me a perfect view of the vast snow-covered world below, the next I could see nothing but swirling dark grey cloud and thick falling snow. Jim came alert immediately. He gave it a short while to see if we'd fly through it then, "no," he said, shaking his head, "it's got nasty out there, I'm going to convert to instruments and re-route, see if I can get down below this cloud. Kids," he shouted, "it's going to be a longer journey than we'd planned I'm afraid. I'm going to try and head around this weather, it's way too hairy for this little plane up here at the moment."

"Nooo," I heard Luke groan, then he yelled, "I'm almost out of battery and my charger's in my suitcase down the back. If we're not landing soon I'm going to have to use your iPad Nate, I'm doing really well, reached level 29, can't leave it now."

"Stay fastened in at the moment," Jim's voice warned to further groans from Luke. "You can worry about iPads when we're out of this mess."

We banked steeply and descended as Jim tried to manoeuvre us out of the snowstorm. He was being ultra-cautious, I knew, we could very probably fly safely right through the blizzard, but Jim wouldn't take a risk when he didn't need to. Why pit your plane against the force of nature when it was a fight you just might not win?!

I switched on the GPS on my iPad and followed us as we changed route, dropped between the hills and headed along a wide valley. After a short while the clouds lightened and became patchy, I could no longer see falling snow. Soon we were back to clear air and a fabulous view of the snaking white valley below.

Jim tried the radio, then shook his head, "no coverage, too far out. We'll need to tell Air Traffic Control we've gone off route as soon as we can." I nodded, the radio only had a range of two hundred miles, and we were in a very remote area. Even if we'd been in range of a tower, we'd have been too low to reach ATC, the signal would have been blocked by the towering hills and mountains on either side of us.

Luke came forward to stand beside me, stretching his back and neck. "Can I have your iPad Nate?" he asked.

"Using it," I replied, waving the GPS map in front of Luke's face. "I'm tracking our route."

"It's clear outside, you don't need to look at where we're going on the iPad, just watch out the window," Luke countered. I opened my mouth, then closed it, there was little point in prolonging the discussion, I'd give in to Luke at some point anyway. Grudgingly I handed my iPad over.

"Cheers Big Ears," grinned Luke, already loading his game as he headed back to his seat.

Suddenly we hit turbulence. The plane dropped and I heard Luke curse behind me as he was pitched forwards, falling with a thud into the aisle. "You okay?" I asked, turning in my seat.

"Umhm," replied Luke, hauling himself up. "More importantly, the iPad's fine," he grinned, brandishing it triumphantly.

I shook my head, chuckling, then gripped my seat as the plane began to buck and bounce violently. Behind me one of the twins gave a little screech.

"Don't worry guys," Jim's calm voice reassured everyone. "Get back in your seat Luke, everyone else just stay where you are, make sure you're strapped in tight. We've hit a patch of clear air turbulence but we should fly out of it pretty soon."

The thing with clear air turbulence is, you can't see it or detect it on radar. In the main, pilots rely on reports from other aircraft and endeavour to fly at an altitude that has been reported as smooth. With so little air traffic over rural Canada however it was easy to fly unexpectedly into rough patches like this.

Flight crews around the world share a common

classification of turbulence: light, moderate and severe. Though it felt terrifying, I guessed this would probably still be classed as light and as such would pose no real worry to Jim. Whilst it seemed as though we were dropping and rising dramatically, I knew we were very likely to be pitching up and down by no more than five, perhaps ten feet. Sure, it was uncomfortable and unpleasant, and I could feel my breakfast bacon, sausage and eggs lurching in my stomach but I knew the turbulence wasn't going to make the plane crash. We were being tossed about like a dinghy on a stormy sea, cresting and dipping over huge waves in the air. but the plane could not be capsized the way a boat could in the water.

Jim's voice continued to be relaxed – "just going to descend to a lower altitude in search of smoother conditions folks. Hopefully we'll be out of this chop in a few minutes." And he was right, no more than ten minutes after it started, we flew out of the rolling, churning swirl and back into smooth air.

"Think you've crushed my hand Sash," I heard Emmi say with a smile in her voice.

"And you've got Malty's fur all squished and matted," added Libby. We all giggled, the high-pitched laughter coming as much from relief as amusement.

Colin came into my mind. I'd always been really scornful of his fear of flying but I felt slightly ashamed of my disdainful dismissiveness now. I'd had my first lesson in the precariousness of flight, I vowed to be more understanding in the future.

I was climbing out of my seat a short while later, to get a drink out of my bag in the cabin when I noticed the sky ahead of us through the cockpit window. We were headed back into low cloud, we wouldn't be able to get down below this, we were already flying along the valley as low as we safely could. I wondered if Jim would re-route again, try a different valley.

Sure enough, as I rooted in my bag in the cabin, I felt us begin to climb and bank once again. Just as well Jim had had that extra fuel put on board, we were all over the place, way off route now. Jim would be referring to his moving map display constantly to navigate, switch our path. We straightened out, presumably down the next valley, though I couldn't confirm this by looking out of the window because the visibility here was just as poor. The clouds swirling round the plane were thick and heavy with snow. Jim would have reverted to instrument flying again, we'd be fine, but I knew he'd prefer to be flying by visual reference.

Luke beckoned to me, I watched him splatting things on his game for a few minutes, making appropriately impressed noises. Then I walked back to the cockpit, "visibility's rubbish again isn't it?" I said to Jim as I came up behind his seat, "do you think we'll come out of this snowstorm any time soon?"

Jim didn't reply, his shoulders had tensed, and I felt a prickle of apprehension. He leaned forward and tapped a dial on the cockpit dashboard. I looked over his shoulder and felt my stomach lurch. I watched, horrified as the needle on the oil pressure gauge dropped steadily. I swivelled my eyes to another dial, seeking reassurance but getting the opposite - as the oil pressure came down, the engine temperature rose.

"Go back and sit down in the cabin Nate," Jim

said evenly enough, though I could hear the anxiety in his voice.

"Best glide speed," he muttered to himself, reaching for the plane's manual as I walked away, "then emergency checklist," he picked up a laminated sheet as I turned on suddenly shaky legs and walked towards the free seat behind Luke. I looked at the others before I sat, observing them in that weird kind of freeze-frame that you see in films before disaster strikes. They were of course, oblivious to our predicament. All were still strapped into their seats. Harvey sat at the back, reading some medical tome, tracing the page with a finger and muttering to himself, his earphones firmly on his head to block out the noise of the flight. Luke was yelping at my iPad, fully absorbed in his game. Emmie was handing sandwiches to the twins. Sasha pushed a drooling Malty off her lap as she grabbed hers and took an enormous bite. I scooped up the small dog and flopped, shell-shocked into a seat as Jim's voice filled the cabin.

"Kids, we've got a problem. It looks like we've got an oil leak, the engine's getting too hot and I'm going to have to shut it down before it seizes. I'm going to bring us down really low to see if I can spot a safe place to land. Make sure your seatbelts are fastened and get into the brace position, it's probably going to get a bit bumpy."

Then, not because he really expected anyone to be flying close enough to hear it, but because it was what was expected of him, he picked up the plane's second radio which was tuned permanently to GUARD, the universal emergency frequency. "Mayday, Mayday, Mayday," he called.

Chapter 5

There was a moment of shocked silence, then a scrabbling as everyone checked and tightened their seat belts and bent forwards, heads between their knees, grasping their shins. I tucked Malty on the seat beside me, keeping one arm firmly around him.

"Jeez," gasped Luke, "we're gonna crash."

Both of the twins wailed loudly. 'Nice one Luke,' I thought as Emmie's low voice carried over to me, trying to calm her little sisters.

"I don't like this, I don't like this," Harvey's booming, panicked voice repeated over and over.

Then suddenly silence, complete and unnatural as Jim shut down the engine and perhaps, like me, everyone's panic gave way to resignation – we were going down, there was nothing we could do about it, the only question was how bad it would be? Would we glide into a safe landing spot smoothly or would we crash? I held my breath, 'please, please, please let us make it down safely.'

I was desperate to look out of the window to see

if the sky was clearing, to see if Jim could get a visual on a safe place to land, to see how close we were to the ground, but I did as I'd been told and stayed bent forward in the brace position. Malty wriggled and although I tried to jam him in with my hip, he slithered free and jumped down. I debated unclipping my belt to grab him again but decided against it, it was every man and dog for himself now.

As we plunged downwards through the swirling grey void, I imagined the plane ripping the fabric of the world, slicing jaggedly through the dense cloud, envisaged it zipping back together behind us. Time stretched, there seemed to be an age of silence, which was probably no more than seconds as we fell. The plane, without an engine, had essentially become a glider and it pitched from side to side, buffeted by the winds and currents in the air. I knew Jim would be watching the air speed indicator, we were going down, he couldn't stop that, but he'd want to minimise the rate of descent, whilst making sure we didn't stall and drop from the sky. He'd been checking the best glide speed in the manual as I'd left the cockpit. He'd be trying to keep us as close to this optimum speed - probably around 65 knots – as he could by lowering or raising the plane's nose. Lowering would speed us up, raising slow us slightly. He'd also be working to keep the wings level to give us the best chance of landing safely, stop us somersaulting as we hit the ground.

Although I couldn't see it, I imagined the ground coming up to meet us, anticipating the crunch of impact. My whole body was tensed and ready, but the first collision came not from the ground - instead we were thrown hard to the right. After the silence and period of seemingly slow-motion descent, everything speeded back up horrifyingly. There was a loud, sickening, ripping sound as something tore at the outer shell of the plane just behind me. The aircraft lurched, the screeching, scraping and thudding continuing outside. It jerked and rocked like a rollercoaster car and in the cabin, chaos reigned. I was thrown around viciously, my shoulder smacked hard against the cabin wall before I was tossed like a rag doll towards the aisle. Unsecured bags flew into the air, most were un-zipped, and their contents became projectiles, flying like cannonballs down the plane, crashing and bouncing along the aisle. A hardback book clipped the side of my head, other less heavy items rained down on me. From the shouting and thudding around me I knew the same thing was happening down the plane. I heard Luke cry out, a startled, pain filled yell, knew he'd been hurt, that something heavy had got him as it shot through the air.

It took me a few seconds to work out what was happening - we were hitting trees. I pictured the dense forested areas I'd seen spread out majestically below when I'd had a clear view of the valley and felt real terror: If we were coming down in the middle of a forest there was almost no chance we'd make it, the trees would tear at the plane until they ripped it to pieces, obliterating all inside.

Miraculously however, it seemed we were falling along the edge of the wooded area. After the first sickening collision and series of scraping and clattering there was again silence. Jim managed to right the plane, the impact had tipped us but not irretrievably, I guessed it may also have slowed our descent slightly, helping us a little perhaps.

Still, we came down fast enough for the plane to torpedo into the snow, hitting the ground with an impact akin to driving into a brick wall at one hundred miles an hour. I pitched hard forward and felt my seatbelt cut agonizingly into my stomach, my nose burst as it slammed into the back of the seat in front of me, warm blood gushed down my face and into my throat as I was thrown backwards again with winding force. I lost the brace position and felt my head crack against my seat, a blackness spread from the corner of my vision and I struggled to remain conscious. We bounced high then smacked back down again, hurtling onwards, the whole aircraft shaking horrifyingly. There was shouting, screaming. I heard one of the twins being sick behind me, then the foul, acid smell of it wound its way up my nose, mingling with the stench of my own blood.

Though I could hear and feel the belly of the plane bump and scrape over bushes and rocks, we hit nothing big on the ground. Just ploughed forwards at an eventually decreasing rate until, with a jerk, we stopped.

For a few seconds I was entirely disoriented, I struggled to process what had just happened – my mind was a whirling, seething mass of thoughts and emotions. Shell-shocked I remained where I was, head between my knees, blood dripping from my face, soaking through my jeans, heart thudding in my chest, breathing loud and ragged. Eventually, my brain analysed the situation, 'the deep snow, that was our salvation, we must have ploughed it ahead of us until the sheer volume of it slowed and eventually stopped our forward trajectory.' My first conscious thought was 'I'm alive,' swiftly followed by my second, 'is anyone else?'

Answering my question, one of the girls began to cry. The acrid smell of sick penetrated my nostrils again, rousing me and dazedly I sat upright. With shaking hands, I fumbled my seatbelt, eventually unclipping it. I staggered upwards and sucked in a sharp breath as the plane seemed to lurch and my vision darkened then brightened. My legs buckled and I grabbed the back of my seat, at first thinking the plane was physically tipping. I realized it wasn't, I had just almost fainted. I closed my eyes briefly, took a few deep breaths then turned around.

The floor of the plane was littered with debris – rucksacks and holdalls trailing their contents, mixed with tablets, phones, books, colouring pencils, sweets, water bottles and bits of sandwiches.

Harvey was still bent forward in his seat, like a frightened hedgehog hiding its head, his hands jammed over his earphones. Emmi was knelt beside the whimpering twins, hugging them tightly to her.

"I've got sick on me," wailed Sasha, "and my mouth tastes yucky."

In front of me, Luke was slumped backwards in his seat, eyes wide with shock. Blood trickled down his chalk-white face and he clutched his right side with his left hand, his right arm lying awkwardly on the armrest of his seat.

"Luke," I gasped, lurching and stumbling towards him. "Are you badly hurt?"

"Maybe, yeah, probably," he muttered through gritted teeth. "I've hurt my arm, well not my arm," he pointed.

"Your collar bone?" I asked and he nodded, "Yeah, I think it might be broken, the girls' Trunkie flew across the cabin and hit me - caught my head first, it's bleeding - then my collar bone. I heard a kind of crunch, I've got a big lump there now. I'm hurt here too," he pulled up his jumper and top and I looked in horror at the side of his chest which was already puffy and purple tinged." It feels like someone is stabbing me with a fork every time I take a breath. I might have broken some ribs"

I knelt beside him but suddenly his eyes went wide and he pushed me aside, surging painfully upwards. He made a noise, a sound I'd not heard made by a human before and lurched, almost passing out, I grabbed him before he fell. His face was sweaty and green tinged, his eyes black pin pricks of pain. "You need to sit back down," I gasped, but Luke shook his head, pushing weakly to get past me.

"My dad," he said. I sucked in my breath, feeling a sudden surge of impending doom: Of course, Jim would have been in immediately to check on us if he could have been, something must be terribly wrong.

I turned, Luke and I stared at the silent cockpit. My feet felt like they were glued to the floor, I knew I had to go and check, but I simply couldn't move. Fear had literally rooted me to the spot. "No," Luke wailed, a desperate prayer. The sound roused my feet to reluctant motion, and I shuffled towards the cockpit on wobbly spaghetti legs, steeling myself for what I'd find. Luke staggered after me, wincing and groaning.

Jim lay slumped over the controls, entirely unmoving. I stood, frozen in the doorway, terrified to move closer to him, scared that I'd touch him and find him already beginning to cool. I felt as though I'd stood up too quickly, all of me seemed to have rushed to the top of my head, lights flickered in front of my eyes and my vision was shimmery. I was …. 'hyperventilating,' the small rational part of me informed the larger freaked-out part, 'cool it Nate, gonna look like a right ass if you keel over here.' I concentrated hard and managed to slow my breathing somewhat, felt a little less faint.

Behind me Luke let out another strangled wail, "Dad, no, please no," he begged again. He tried to push past, but I blocked him with my arm, he couldn't be the one to do this. Gingerly I leant forward and placed the first two fingers of my other hand on Jim's neck.

A beat, two, I sagged forwards, letting out a huge sigh of relief, "he's alive but, I can't see anything whilst he's flopped over the controls." I turned to Luke, "I know you won't want to, but you can't help me, please move back so Emmie can get in to help me lie your dad back against the seat."

Luke did as I'd asked. I stuck my head out of the cockpit and beckoned to Emmi. She was holding a Tupperware in front of Sasha. Sasha was gargling water noisily and badly, flapping her hands and gagging, almost making herself vomit again, then spitting into the box.

Emmie, put down the Tupperware, gave the twins a last hug and came over to me. As she got closer I could see she was sporting a bloody nose to match my own. In the enclosed space of the cockpit, we manoeuvred ourselves to either side of Jim and very, very gently eased him backwards.

Now that I could see him, I could tell

immediately where his problem lay –he'd hit his head on the coaming, the sun shield over the instrument panel. His forehead was gashed badly above his left eye, there was a lot of blood and already a large purple swelling. Ooh, blood, gore, nasty! I was totally freaked out by the situation, teetering dangerously on the edge of a complete melt-down.

"What's wrong? How bad is he," Luke's shrill voice forced me to give myself a hefty mental-shake. I took a big gulp of air and assessed the situation more rationally, keeping myself deliberately turned away from Luke - there was no need for him to see the panic and horror in my eyes.

The cut on Jim's head was nasty, ragged, about 4cm in length but the blood was already beginning to clot. He'd clearly been knocked out, but he could come round soon and in the meantime, he wasn't about to bleed to death. "He's hit his head. Hard, but I think he'll be okay."

Luke nodded and sagged forwards. "Whoa," I shouted, lurching to grab him before he fell. He cried out as I caught his arm. He was ashen and his face had a sweaty sheen, his eyes were dark pools of pain. I think the only thing keeping him upright had been concern for his dad. "We need to get you sat back down." I supported him back to the nearest seat, the one he'd been in when we crashed.

In the seats behind, the twins clung to each other, their identical eyes wide and frightened. "Is Mr Carter dead?" whispered Libby.

"No," I replied, trying for a reassuring smile. "He's just banged his head, he's knocked himself out, but he'll be fine."

Sasha suddenly pushed herself out of her sister's arms and began looking around frantically, "Malty?" she cried.

Oh no! I'd not seen the little dog since he'd jumped off my seat before the crash, a quick scan of the cockpit didn't locate him. The threads of fear began to creep within me again, like fast-growing weeds. We were lurching from one horror to the next. I wasn't sure I could deal with much more and jeez, why did it seem like I was the one taking control here, that wasn't what I did, no way, I was a follower, not a leader - Luke's friend Nate, nothing more! Hyperventilating once again, fearing the worst I got to my knees and scanned under the seats. Malty lay in the footwell of Emmie's seat, merrily munching a mangled heap of sandwich. I let out a mortifying sound that was halfway between a laugh and a sob, cut it off by shoving my fist in my mouth then leaned behind Sasha and scooped the dog up, depositing him, still greedily gulping down egg and bread, on her knee.

"Oh Malty," Sasha gasped burying her face in his wiry fur and bursting into noisy tears.

We stood or sat where we were for what seemed like an age, all lost in our own private thoughts. In a foggy daze of shock, my mind dashed haphazardly through the crash, trying to process and make sense of what had occurred, decide what we should do now. I couldn't grab hold of anything, couldn't pluck anything even vaguely constructive from my brain, the trauma was making my thoughts flit uselessly. I gave up and sank to the floor, closing my eyes, listening to Sasha's sobbing, fighting tears myself.

Chapter 6

"So, what do we do now?" Emmi asked some time later, coming up beside me.

I gaped at her, opening and shutting my mouth like a fish. Faced with any decision, let alone one as fundamental as this, I'd habitually begin my reply with 'I'm not sure.' I'm more than a little erratic, never quite confident enough to form my own opinion, always unduly influenced by others and likely to change my mind at the drop of a hat. I was hardly Disaster Lead Officer material! 'No, no, no, not the decision maker, not me, go away, get someone else to take the lead,' I yelled in my head.

Realistically though, I knew there was no one else: Jim was unconscious; Luke was too badly hurt; Emmi had her sisters to look after and Harvey wouldn't be up to the job. I opened my mouth, but Harvey's booming voice cut me off. "We wait to be rescued. When we don't call Whitehorse within an hour of our expected landing time they'll issue a MANOT."

"A Missing Aircraft Notice," I translated flatly.

"Not the time to show off your aviation knowledge Nate," spat Luke. I turned to him stunned, totally wrong-footed by the fury in his voice. His face displayed a raging storm of anger and pain and for an instant I wished I were Harvey and had a legitimate reason to avoid looking into it. The foul mood sat all wrong on him, my sunny natured friend.

"I, I wasn't," I stammered, my voice pleading, wheedling, like I was trying to coax an angry toddler from its tantrum, "I was just…"

"Well just don't, no one here is impressed," he cut me off nastily.

The world went blurry, watery, and my throat clogged as tears prickled my eyes. 'Oh no. Oh hell,' I couldn't cry in front of them all. I looked at my feet and gulped in great breaths.

"So, a rescue team should come for us soon?" Emmi came to my aid kindly.

I nodded, partly because I couldn't speak and partly because I couldn't bring myself to voice my concerns. I worried how effective that MANOT would be. Sure, they'd realise we were missing when we failed to put down and make that phone call in Old Crow, but we were way off route and had not been able to get radio coverage to notify Air Traffic Control. It was far too remote up here for radar coverage - no one had been tracking our flight. To make matters worse, the storm we'd hit in the air continued to rage around us. Whilst they were well prepared for difficult rescue scenarios in Canada, even having a specialist parachute section to deploy to remote, difficult to access areas, they'd be unlikely to mount a search in this. They'd not risk more lives for the sake of some that might well already be terminated.

To give myself time to calm down I searched the cabin floor for my iPad. I'd check the GPS, find out where we were at least. I dropped to my knees, my iPad lay under one of the seats, alongside Luke's phone, the screens on both were smashed. I wasn't going to be able to look at anything on either of those. Luke's iPad was, of course, dead.

"Anyone got an iPad or phone I can use to get our location?" I asked when it felt safe to speak. Everyone shook their heads. Emmi waggled her Kindle, that was the only device she had, the girls had portable DVD players.

"I don't do technology," boomed Harvey. "Too bright and loud and fast and flashy."

"Does your dad have one," I addressed Luke cautiously. I'd never seen Jim with one, but it was possible he'd just never used it in my company. Luke, slumped in his seat, shook his head without opening his eyes to look at me.

Great! "Oh well," I sighed, completely forgetting the plane had GPS linked to its moving map display, "I guess it doesn't really matter." In all honesty, I knew that looking at the GPS would do no more than confirm what I already knew – we were somewhere close to nowhere, marooned in our own private wilderness. Surrounded by nothing other than mile upon square mile of nature in its rawest, most elemental form.

"Can we contact anyone?" Emmi asked. "Will someone have picked up Jim's Mayday call?"

"Mayday," lectured Harvey, "from the French m'aidez, meaning help me."

Luke snorted, I really hoped he wasn't going to have a go at poor Harvey too. "I don't think so," I replied quickly, "they'd have responded immediately if they had."

"We can put out a radio call on the emergency frequency – 121.5," replied Harvey.

Again, I kept my thoughts to myself. He was right, we could, and I would, it was worth a try but I knew that the reason Jim hadn't notified Air Traffic Control about our changed route was because we weren't within the two-hundred-mile range necessary for radio contact. That even if we had been, the radio needed uninterrupted line of sight to work, we were tucked at the bottom of a valley, no way that signal would get out past the hills and forests. Of course, if someone flew over our valley we could reach them but that wasn't likely to happen in this weather.

"There's also the ELT," said Harvey. Good point, there would be an Emergency Locator Transmitter in the cockpit, if it were armed it would have begun to transmit on impact, I'd need to check its status, make sure it was in fact turned on. The ELT

would transmit on two frequencies: a civil frequency -
which it would do continuously for at least the next
fifty hours - emitting a distinctive, high pitched distress
signal that would shriek loudly into the headsets of any
other pilots in our area; and via satellite for the
following twenty-four hours. Like the radio, the
transmission on the civil frequency would be unlikely
to be picked up because we'd be outside anyone's
range but the distress call via satellite would have been
received, satellites were everywhere these days. The
rescue co-ordination centre monitoring SARSAT – the
search and rescue satellite system - wouldn't be in
Canada, there were only a handful in the world, but
they'd notify the Canadian Centre as soon as they
picked up our distress signal. The problem with the
satellite was that it would only provide a rescuer with a
very broad, generalised location. Someone would know
we were down, but they wouldn't really know where to
look, even when the weather allowed them to.

In the small cockpit, I wriggled myself round
Jim and located the ELT, the LED light was flashing, it
was transmitting. Next, I spent ten minutes trying the

radio before giving up, mourning the lack of a Sat Phone – few small planes had them, they were too expensive – but we really could have done with one.

"No luck reaching anyone yet," I informed the others, walking down the cabin. "The best thing we can do for now is get some extra clothes on, it's going to get really cold in here pretty quickly."

Emmi and I clambered over the detritus in the aisle to where our luggage was stored, behind a net in the back of the plane. The suitcases were battered, lying in a heap, tangled with skis, snowboards, boot bags and helmets. We dragged them out one by one, some had been smashed with such force against the side of the plane they'd actually cracked open. I pulled thick jumpers, hats, gloves and ski jackets from Luke's and my case and a jacket and salopettes from Jim's. I didn't want to move Jim too much, certainly didn't want to try to pull jumpers over his head, I reckoned the best we could do would be to pull his coat around his shoulders and cover his legs with his thick ski pants.

"Argh," Emmi cried. I looked over at her, she was rooting around in Libby's case. She held up a clear zipped bag full of small vials, most of them broken. "Libby's insulin," she said, "she's diabetic. Still, I suppose there'll be a hospital in Old Crow, we'll be able to get some more from there, there's still a few days' worth here."

I said nothing, I really hoped I was wrong about them struggling to rescue us.

Luke snatched the extra clothes from me with his good hand, still not speaking. He looked horrifyingly un-Luke like. His face was haggard, tense and drawn. His shiny blonde hair was dark and sticky with sweat. Even his usually bright blue eyes had lost their spark and dimmed. I stared at him in horror, it looked like something had eaten his soul. The strained silence roared around the two of us.

"What," he snapped at last. I opened my mouth but couldn't think of anything to say to this new, terrifying Luke, I just shook my head and moved away.

When we were all dressed more warmly and Jim was wrapped up as best as we could manage, Emmi suggested we take a look outside. I looked out of the window sceptically, the snow bleached down still and the wind gusted strongly enough to rock the small plane.

"We can try." Harvey stayed in his seat as did Luke. Emmi and the girls clustered around me, Sasha hugging Malty, as I wrestled with the cabin door, fighting a battle with the wind as I pushed out and it pushed in. During a split-second lull, I won, and the door flew open, a barrage of hard, icy snow blasted in on fridge cold air, covering us all, the wind nearly knocking us off our feet. I gasped and lurched for the open door, dragging it shut as quickly as I could.

I looked at the girls, their surprised, wide eyed expressions must have mirrored my own. Each of us was sprayed with snow, Malty was covered too, he'd scrabbled frantically up Sasha's shoulder and clung to her like a large, hairy parrot. She pulled him down and he dropped to the floor, scooting down the plane, ears flat and tail tucked in. His fur had clumped in icy spikes. "He's a hedgedog," giggled Libby.

"A dogupine," countered Sasha. We laughed then, uproariously. Of course, it wasn't really funny, the situation was dire, the weather far worse than I'd feared, but we looked ridiculous, shocked rigid, snow clinging to our fronts so completely it looked like we'd been spray painted with sparkling white emulsion. Harvey joined in, his laugh was louder than his speaking voice and it resounded round the confined cabin. Even Luke opened his eyes and managed a small smile.

Chapter 7

We dusted ourselves down and Emmi and I headed down the plane to where Harvey sat to see if we could persuade him to take a look at Jim and Luke, use his medical knowledge to give a prognosis. He adamantly refused, got a bit upset when I tried to push.

"He loves medicine," Emmi explained, "and will study text books and journals all day long but as he's told you he could never be a doctor – says he doesn't want to see the real stuff, that if he looks at real injuries or sees real pain he'll never get it out of his head. It won't do any good to make him look, he won't be able to handle it. He can view any amount of gore in his books and be fascinated, actual injury will just freak him out."

"Okay," I agreed reluctantly, not really understanding but accepting her explanation, nevertheless. I pondered for a moment. "If I describe Jim and Luke's injuries to you instead Harvey, can you tell me what you know about their conditions, how bad they are, whether there's anything we should be doing for them?"

"Sure," Harvey perked up instantly. It had become a hypothetical situation for him and suddenly he was interested rather than repulsed.

I started with Luke, described how his arm was hanging unnaturally from the shoulder, how he was badly bruised and hurting down one side with sharp pains when he breathed.

"Sounds like he's broken his collar bone and cracked or broken some ribs," Harvey confirmed Luke's self-diagnosis.

"The collar bone or clavicle is a large, curved bone that connects the arm to the body," he lectured happily. "In most cases the bone will snap in the middle where it is thinnest, but it is possible to break the bone in several places at once. A complicated break may require surgery to realign the bone, a simple break will hurt and should be strapped to keep it immobile. It will take six to eight weeks to heal but much longer for full strength to be restored to the shoulder. Physical therapy is necessary to ensure a patient retains full use of the arm."

Wow, he was a talking medical textbook, he clearly had a photographic memory and really knew his stuff.

Emmi waved the scarf she'd been using to stem them blood from her nose, "scarf," she suggested, "to strap Luke's arm, just, umm," she wriggled the bloody item with distaste, "not this one."

"So," I summarised, "the broken collar bone is not dangerous but does need x-raying as soon as possible in case it needs to be set."

"Correct," replied Harvey, "and Luke should see a physio as soon as he can, get advice on what to do or not to do or his arm may always be stiff and not fully mobile."

"Right, what about his ribs?"

"Luke's ribs could be cracked or they could be broken," he repeated. "Whilst still painful, cracked ribs aren't as dangerous as ribs that have been broken into separate pieces. A jagged edge of broken bone can easily damage major blood vessels or internal organs, such as the lung, especially if it becomes displaced."

Oh, oh, that sounded worrying. "What does

displaced mean?"

"If the rib has moved. The more broken ribs there are, the more dangerous it is. The only way to know how many ribs Luke has damaged and whether they are cracked or broken, in-place or displaced is to X-ray, it should be done immediately"

"Well obviously it can't be," I squawked, waving my arms at the walls of the cabin, panicked again, trying not to get annoyed. "Is there anything we can do to help?"

Harvey thought for a moment, "Stop him moving around too much and give him pain relief. It'll hurt when he breathes, if he doesn't breathe deeply enough, mucous and moisture can build up in his lungs and lead to an infection such as pneumonia. Keep him medicated so that he continues to breathe sufficiently deeply. Don't strap his chest, it'll only restrict his breathing further. The swelling can be reduced by holding an ice pack to the affected area."

'No ice packs but plenty of lumps of ice outside if we can ever get out there,' I thought. I looked at Emmi, "have any of you got any painkillers?" She shook her head.

"Oh, actually I have," I remembered. Mum had slipped them in my wash bag in case I got a headache, or a sore throat, or earache, or lord knows what other ailment!

"Shall I get them out of your suitcase," Emmi asked. I nodded and she clambered back to the luggage and began rummaging through my bag.

"The good news is, most broken ribs heal themselves within a couple of months," continued Harvey.

A couple of months, fantastic!! I blew out a deep breath.

"Right, how about Jim then," I said. "He's got a big gash on his forehead, his eye and the bit above it is purple and swollen. He's out cold, we can't get any response from him at all."

"Brain injury," said Harvey authoritatively. "When the brain is injured it tends to swell, but, unlike most parts of your body, it doesn't have anywhere to go because the skull is a small space. Inflammation can cause the brain to push up against the skull and increase pressure. "It's good news Mr Carter is in a coma really," he mused. "Doctors often put patients with brain injuries in medically-induced comas to allow the brain to rest, make sure that it does not exert itself any more than necessary. He lent back his head and closed his eyes in a 'man-in-a-coma' simulation. "If the brain is kept quiet, the healing process can occur slowly and naturally, the swelling should reduce, there's less chance of intracranial pressure building up and brain cells being damaged. Doctors cool the bodies of patients with brain injuries too, to slow brain activity even further.

"Cool to what temperature?" I asked.

"32-34 degrees."

"Right," I said, I'd need to get those ski clothes I'd just put on him back off. "So, we keep Jim cold and don't try to rouse him. When will he wake up though?"

"Impossible to say - in a minute, an hour, a week, who knows? Oh, you should check his pupils, shine a torch on them. If they react to the light he'll probably be okay. Only twenty percent of patients with a brain injury with reactive pupils die," he concluded cheerfully.

"Right," I said faintly. "I'll get on to that now."

The torch I found in the cockpit was a huge lantern style device. Probably not the thing to use - if Jim's brain needed rest it wouldn't take kindly to being shocked into reaction by an enormous blinding beam being shone in his eye. A quick discussion and further scrabble through the suitcases turned up Libby's small, clip over, reading light.

Emmi and I approached the cockpit, "What you doing?" asked Luke in a bullying voice. It didn't worry me this time, I could tell it was just masking the fear he was feeling.

"Just checking something," I replied as brightly as I could. "Nothing to worry about."

Emmi gently prised open Jim's eyelids whilst I shone the pen size light in his eye, both of us craning forwards, heads squashed together to see whether his pupils were a normal size and reacted to the light. They were and they did. Emmi and I grinned, then high fived each other ridiculously – a comatose man was not really cause for celebration, but Jim's situation was less bad than it could have been. You've got to be thankful for small mercies right?

Emmi nipped out to tell Luke the 'good' news whilst I dragged the layers I'd just heaped on Jim back off.

I used the brief moment alone to process my thoughts. Everyone else was fully expecting to be rescued today. I was fairly certain that wasn't going to happen and, though I tried to ignore it, a very determined voice in my head told me it may not be tomorrow, or anytime in the near future. The weather charts had shown today as being the best to travel, a small window of decent weather in an otherwise terrible couple of weeks. Sure, they'd been wrong about today, but it didn't mean tomorrow wouldn't be worse. Certainly, a rescue party would come across us eventually. Once the weather cleared they'd start along our planned route then widen the search from there until eventually someone flew over and either picked up our ELT signal before the battery died or spotted us on the ground. But when would they get here? When would this storm clear? And once this one passed how much search time would they get before another one grounded the team again? If we'd all been physically okay we could sit it out and wait for help to get here but we weren't all okay - Jim and Luke required urgent medical attention and Libby's insulin would only get her through a few days. Was there a chance one or more of them would actually die before someone reached us?

They were extremely worrying questions, but I was suddenly exhausted, zapped of all energy. For now, I didn't want to consider them, I just wanted to do what everyone else was doing and settle down quietly and wait.

So that's what I did, what we did. We strapped Luke's arm with a scarf, filled him with some painkillers and wrapped him up. He sat silent and stony faced through it all, barely managing to control his seething, bubbling anger. Emmi and I took turns to check Jim periodically to see if there was any change in his condition. We didn't have a thermometer, so we monitored his temperature, no doubt very inaccurately, by touch. Keeping him on the chilly side of cool but not letting him get too cold, putting extra layers on, then stripping them back off. I glued my face to the window every ten minutes or so, searching for any sign the snowstorm was winding up.

Darkness fell rapidly, there are very few hours of daylight this far north. Gloomy and dusk like anyway, the stormy day soon descended into night. By 4.30pm, three and a half hours after we'd crashed, it was pitch black outside. Emmi had come up with the idea of hanging the lantern torch from the back of the cockpit door. We'd used the belt from her salopettes, and the cabin was bathed in dim light. We'd tried the radio at regular intervals, though the rational part of me knew it was pointless. Still, I wasn't ready to acknowledge we'd need to spend the night here with two of our number badly injured, nor ready to explain to the others why there was no hope of a quick resolution to our dire situation.

Sasha was the first to say it out loud, "they'll not come for us in the dark will they," she enquired, voice wobbling a little.

"No," I answered reluctantly when no one else spoke up. "We're going to have to stay here, make ourselves as comfortable as possible."

"I can't sleep in the same place as anyone else," boomed Harvey, his voice even louder than usual, emphasising there could be no compromise on this position. "I need to be on my own."

I looked at Emmi for inspiration. Shadowy in the torchlight, she cupped her chin in her hands, squinted her eyes and thought for a few minutes.

"How about we make a barrier with the suitcases, just behind the cargo net? You can snuggle down behind there and it'll be just like having your own little room," she said, trying to make it sound appealing.

"It'll be dark," replied Harvey, unconvinced, "I can't be in the dark."

Emmi glanced wistfully at the torch, without it the rest of us would be in complete darkness. "You can take the torch," she said.

So that's what happened, Harvey squeezed himself into the tail of the plane, torch in hand and we made a wall of suitcases round him. Then we curled in a seat each, listening to the storm raging in the dark.

Chapter 8

Against all odds, everyone around me slept. I sighed and closed my eyes, willing myself to sleep too. At some point in the night I must have drifted off and woke, as the sky began to lighten from black to murky grey, cold, stiff and sore. The others slept on, though not peacefully. Emmi's head was thrashing from side to side, in the grip of some awful dream. The twins whimpered and muttered, and Luke was moaning softly in his sleep. There was no sign, nor sound from Harvey. Quietly, painfully I stood up and walked, with some apprehension towards Jim. He lay still as stone in exactly the position we'd left him. I tentatively reached out my hand and touched his cheek, his skin was cold, and I feared the worst but when I wriggled my finger under his shirt collar and pressed it to his neck I felt a pulse.

"Is he alive?" Emmi's voice, though she whispered so as not to wake anyone, startled me and I jumped. "Sorry," she said, giving a small, half smile, then her eyes widened, "whoa," she said at exactly the same time as me.

I raised my hand to my eyes, "black?"

"Yup," she nodded, "well, purple actually, both of them."

"Yours too," I grinned, "snap." She looked nervously back at Jim.

"It's OK," I reassured her, "he's cold though, too cold possibly. I'm going to wrap him up for a while."

I arranged a collection of clothing over Jim, tucking it round him as best I could.

"The storm's passed," said Emmi. I'd thought of nothing but Jim, but she was right, the howling wind and lashing, icy snow were no more. The cloud was still right down around us, but a weak beam of sunshine was strobing through and beginning to seep in through the windows of the plane.

"Shall we take a look outside?"

"Let's wake the others first," Emmi replied, "I don't want the twins frightened if they wake and find I'm not there."

Emmi gently roused the twins and headed off

towards Harvey, whilst I woke Luke. I watched the confusion in his eyes when he first opened them quickly turn to fear as he jolted upright, clutching his arm with a cry. He lurched towards his father. "It's OK," I said pushing him gently back in his seat. "Your Dad's alive but he still hasn't come round yet. You should try to stay still." But Luke pushed me roughly aside and rose shakily to his feet, going over to Jim and putting his finger to his neck as I'd done. He gave a little nod before stumbling back and collapsing once again in his seat.

"You've got black eyes Emmi," I heard Sasha giggle. "Ooh, you too Nate, you're like a pair of pandas."

"It's the look of the season," I replied. "Just wait, when the world sees us they'll be bashing their faces on seat backs right, left and centre to get the same." The girls all laughed.

"Ow," moaned Emmi, holding her nose, "laughing hurts."

"The storm's stopped," I said to Luke, "Emmi and I are going to take a look outside." Luke nodded but didn't reply, his face was tight with pain. I handed him some painkillers and he gulped them down with some water.

Emmi left the twins and, trailed by Harvey - who emerged from his lair with the hair on one side of his head standing straight in the air in a gravity defying way - joined me at the door. I pushed it open and we all squashed together, peering out.

One by one, we stepped out, there was no need to lower the steps, the plane had ploughed itself a groove and sat deep in the hard, sparkling snow. The freezing early morning air burned my swollen nose as I breathed it in. I turned around slowly, taking in the scene around me. The day was struggling to get light - giving it its best shot but just falling short. Through the grey gloom I could see that my assumption that the plane had acted like a snow plough, pushing more and more snow in front of itself, until finally it was brought to a stop by a great mound in front of its nose, was correct. It rested on the top of a bank which led to a frozen lake. Behind the plane a deep scar cut raggedly through the snow, this had been partially refilled by last night's heavy fall.

We'd been incredibly lucky I realised, the trees we'd hit were at the very edge of a thick forest, if we'd come down farther to the left we'd have crashed into the heart of it. The plane would almost certainly have been torn to pieces, killing us all. As it was, although dented and scraped, the plane looked in remarkably good shape. I walked its length; the worst of the damage was at the back. That made sense, the impact I'd heard and felt had been behind my seat on the plane.

I returned to Emmi and Harvey as the twins climbed down from the plane, blinking, pulling their coats tight around them. "Ooh, it's cold," gasped Sasha. She was carrying Malty as usual, but the dog wriggled and jumped from her arms, landing with a soft whoomph in the snow, sinking right to his belly, leaving behind his imprint – a perfect snow doggy-angel, as he scrambled back out. He snuffled and frolicked, scooting over the hard snow, trailing tiny footprints like ink blots on a piece of crisp white paper, tail tucked in and ears flat, sinking into the softer drifts, disappearing for a moment before hauling himself back out. We all burst out laughing, his joy at being outside, perhaps even at being alive – who knew how much dogs understood - was infectious. Soon the girls and I were all whooping, charging about, feet creaking and crunching in the snow as we hurled armfuls at one another. Harvey stood with his hands clamped on his ears to block out our noise, but he grinned along with us. We'd cheated death, were invincible, we were celebrating.

"They'll come for us today won't they?" asked Sasha, when we'd exhausted ourselves and stood, bent forward, hands on knees, blowing hard.

Not telling them my fears was one thing, lying was another. Everyone was suddenly serious, looking at me. "I'm not sure," I said, "the weather's much better than yesterday but the cloud is still very thick, at least at ground level, it's impossible to say whether it's any clearer up high, whether they'll be able to fly above it." I took a deep breath, I'd started so I might as well get it all off my chest, "also, we were way off route when we went down, Jim couldn't tell anyone because we're in too remote an area for radio coverage, no one really knows where we are. They'll look for us whenever the weather allows but it may take them some time to find us."

"What do you mean by some time?" asked Emmi. I could see from her face she was picturing the depleted supply of insulin.

"Anyone's guess. As I already said, the weather will play a major factor, might stop anyone searching at all. If they can search I've no idea how quickly they might locate us."

"Hmm," said Harvey cheerfully, "that's okay, I like it here, it's beautiful, and lovely and quiet." We all looked around us, I suppose in different circumstances I might have agreed. At this point in time however all I could see was terrifying bleakness and isolation and in my mind's eye, a truly hideous slide show of rescuers loading three dead bodies onto the search and rescue helicopter.

Emmi's stricken face told me she was envisaging the same thing. "Is there anything we can do?" she asked.

I floundered; I was way out of my comfort zone

here. Since we'd first met, Luke had organised our lives so completely that I never had to come up with ideas or plans of my own. I wasn't sure I was capable of identifying possibilities, let alone coming up with solutions. She stared at me, waiting and I stared back, helplessly. At last she gave a snort and shook her head slightly, the corner of her mouth lifting in a small sneer. Turning she walked back towards the plane, the girls trooping solemnly after her.

I had let her down and I felt rotten.

"I like it here," repeated Harvey following them, merrily oblivious to everyone else's despair.

"Light a beacon," commanded Luke. He'd picked up on our despondency when we'd got back on-board. Emmi had explained my concern and he had jumped in with both feet, lobbing out a tornado of ideas at full force. "Start walking, launch some flares, keep trying the radio, get the locator thingy to high ground"

"We have no flares, I replied, "I will keep trying the radio, but it won't be any good unless someone flies right over us."

"Collect some wood then, get a beacon going.

Then start climbing with the locator, when you reach one of the peaks you'll be able to look for a road."

I knew none were good solutions, to see a fire someone would need to be flying overhead, if they were flying overhead they'd pick up our ELT signal anyway, or our radio call. Getting the ELT to high ground was a good idea in theory, it's signal would not be blocked up there as it would down here and would carry over a much greater range, but the peaks at either side of the valley were huge. The area held some of Canada's highest mountains, they were rocky, snowy and tree covered, I couldn't just nip to the top, I'd need climbing gear to get up them. Finally, it was very unlikely there'd be a road, there just weren't really any around here, less likely would be finding one in use at this time of year. At a rough guess, we were a hundred miles from the airfield at which we'd refuelled. A hundred miles was walkable in theory, but only over the course of a few days. In the freezing temperatures and thick snow, I couldn't just camp out en-route, I'd die of exposure, probably on the first night. Also, the hundred-mile estimate was as the crow flies, how far

I'd have to walk to get out of the valley was anyone guess. I realised Luke had not really put any thought into any of his suggestions – he was just, in his usual infinitely restless manner, bouncing like a whirlwind from one thing to another.

Still, conditioned to unquestioning obedience, I found myself pulling on extra layers and thick gloves and heading out the door with the Fallons to begin gathering wood.

We weren't a huge distance from the forest. We walked as far as we could in the trench dug by the plane, then waded the last few hundred meters through thigh deep snow. It was hard going, there were patches where the snow was hard packed, and you sunk in very little but also many patches of drift - soft and sinky as quicksand.

The plane had brought down several branches, which were just visible under the newly fallen snow and we collected those first with ease, dragging the large ones and carrying the small ones a safe distance from the forest edge before making a pile. After that, it became more difficult, there were thousands of trees, but they were huge firs, their branches beginning twenty feet above the ground, snow hanging rather beautifully in sleeves of white along their length. After slogging for over an hour we still had a pathetically small beacon. I reckoned it might burn for a couple of hours – much use that would be!!

Whilst we worked, the sun, filtering patchily through the clouds, faded. The cloud became more dense and fine snow began to fall. The white-on white made foot/eye coordination tricky, it became impossible to work out where the ground ended, and sky began. We simply couldn't see where we were placing our feet, and with increasing frequency we stumbled, misjudging our step.

"No one's going to be flying around here in this are they?" asked Emmi. I shook my head. "There's no point in lighting a beacon yet then. Shall we give up for now, come back out if the weather improves?"

We floundered blindly back to the plane. As we climbed in I knocked something with my foot, the painkillers. I bent down and picked up the packet, there were just over half left, there'd been a full packet yesterday afternoon – twenty-four tablets.

"How many of these have you been taking?" I asked Luke, waving them in front of him.

"Just two at a time," he replied flatly, the life had drained even from his voice, he spoke now in a slow, dull monotone.

"Yeah, but how often?" I pushed.

Luke shrugged dismissively "what's that got to do with you?" he challenged. I didn't back down, just continued to stare at him. "Jeez, I dunno," he answered at last, "when the pain gets really bad I just take them and it eases a bit, when it comes back I take some more."

"Aw Luke," I sighed, "you overdosing is the last thing we need, and these are all the pills we've got. I know you're in pain," I touched his good shoulder, I really was sympathetic, "but you're going to have to slow down."

"You going to try and find a road?" he replied petulantly. "So that we can get out of here and not have to worry about the limited supply of painkillers?"

'No,' I said in my head, 'it's a fool's quest. I

wouldn't know which direction to head in even if I could see, I certainly won't be able to work out where to go in the complete white-out out there.'

"Soon," I replied, "just going to find something to eat first, I'm hungry, are you?" As I said it, I realised that I wasn't just hungry, I was absolutely ravenous. With the exception of the girls having a couple of bites of sandwich just before the plane came down, none of us had eaten since breakfast yesterday morning.

Luke shook his head, "Not really, feel a bit sick actually."

This was worrying, the Luke I knew was perpetually hungry. "Pills might be turning your stomach," I said, "soaking them up with some food might be a good thing."

Luke just shrugged. "Let's see what we've got to eat," I said to the Fallons.

Jim's suitcase turned out to be a positive food treasure trove. Luke's Mum had packed a load of 'English Goodies the Fallons might not be able to get in Canada.' We rooted the items out from amongst the clothes and toiletries and piled them in the aisle.

There were:

2 packs of Carrs' Water Biscuits.

2 packs of McVitie's Digestives, 1 plain, 1 chocolate.

2 Jars of Fortnum and Mason Jam, one raspberry, one strawberry.

2 packs of Hobnobs.

A giant bar of Cadbury's Milk Chocolate.

A tin of Bird's Custard Powder.

A large pack of Warbuton's Crumpets.

Beef Oxo Cubes.

2 bars of Kendal Mint Cake, 1 plain, 1 chocolate.

A box of Earl Grey Tea.

I added Gummi Bears, Cola Bottles, two cans of Fanta and salt and vinegar Pringles from my bag, and two Pain Aux Chocolate I'd stolen from the breakfast buffet at the hotel. Jelly Bellies, cheese Doritos, mint humbugs and a bottle of Lucozade from Luke's. From the plane's emergency box, I pulled a large packet of boiled sweets and half a dozen bottles of water.

Emmi, somewhat smugly I thought, contributed

unsalted almonds, banana chips, a tub of mixed seeds, a box of fruit and oat bars, and four more bottles of water. She sheepishly added a selection of fruit, also stolen from breakfast. Harvey hugged his rucksack to him, looked shifty and handed over nothing.

"Harvey only really likes red food," explained Libby, "he'll need to keep what he's got." Harvey nodded, squirreling his rucksack away under his seat.

Okaay! … Still, a decent haul! I stuffed a slightly stale Pain Aux Chocolate in my mouth and took the other one to Luke, along with his bottle of Lucozade. He unenthusiastically ate a few bites, washed them down with a gulp of Lucozade and looked at me pointedly.

"Heading out now," I said. "Can I borrow your gloves? Mine are soaking from collecting wood."

As soon as I got out of the plane, I began mentally kicking myself for not having the courage to say no to Luke. There were no roads. I knew that and the futile quest would become positively dangerous in these conditions. The visibility was shockingly poor, a blurred world encased in a veil of low cloud. With no visual points of reference, I'd soon lose all sense of direction and get lost.

I stood for a few moments, trying to pluck up the courage to get back on the plane and tell Luke I wasn't going. It was actually nice being outside I decided, on my own, without a thousand dramas unfolding around me. I would take a few minutes to clear my head.

Something that had been puzzling me, but which I'd not really had a chance to give any 'thought time' to was what had caused the plane to crash? I pictured the dials - oil, we'd run out of oil, but why? The engineer had confirmed he'd just changed the oil, Jim would have noticed if he had emptied and failed to refill the tank sufficiently. We must have had enough oil when we took off, what could have caused us to lose it? A leak in the tank, the sump, was possible but unlikely, the engineer would have noticed weak spots on the metal - any rusted area that could have turned into a hole. Also, the leak had been rapid? Whilst, a tiny rusted area going unnoticed was just about possible, one large enough to allow oil to run out so rapidly was very unlikely to have been missed.

The engineer had been working on something under the cowling when we'd arrived. I walked to the front of the plane, there was a sticky liquid all down the fuselage – oil. I unfastened the clasps and pulled at the flap. It was frozen shut, but I managed to jiggle it loose. Yup, oil everywhere. The filter was lying in the bottom of the engine compartment.

Footage of Colin in his garage played on a reel in my mind. He'd been fitting an oil filter to a car last weekend when I'd been 'helping' him at work. He'd screwed it on with his hand but had used a wrench to tighten it. What if the plane engineer had not done this? He'd had a wrench in his hand but perhaps he'd hand screwed the filter then had been distracted by us turning up at the plane, or by his phone call. Maybe he'd forgotten to wrench the filter tight. We'd hit turbulence not long before we became aware of the problem, the jolting and juddering of the plane could have been enough to dislodge the loose filter.

A tiny seed of an idea began to germinate in my mind. Hmm, I'd need some time to think this through, but I was getting cold just standing here. I could walk and think, I was about to head along the furrow the plane had dug in the snow, it was relatively easy going and I'd not lose my way, when I had another thought, I could head across the frozen lake. If I was to develop my wisp of a plan, the length of the lake would be relevant, I couldn't see the far bank, but then I could barely see my hand if I stuck out my arm. I could walk on the lake, get a rough feel for its size and think at the same time, kill two birds with one stone.

I slithered down the steep bank onto the lake, there was just enough snow on it to stop it being too slippery but not enough to make it difficult to walk. Why was the snow less thick on the lake than on the ground I wondered – did it just freeze on here, building up the ice crust? Did the wind blow it straight off? I couldn't see enough to work out if I was crossing the lake at its widest point, but I started to walk, shuffling my feet along to make a track in the snow. It wasn't snowing at the moment, I reckoned I could walk out then turn and follow my tracks back to the plane and not get lost.

I'd been shuffling and thinking for about ten minutes and was starting to get a good feeling about the length of the lake when something off to the left caught my eye. The faintest outline of something dark standing out in the white world.

I changed course, kept up my shuffling motion and headed towards the shape. The plan I was beginning to formulate was forgotten for the moment. I smiled then grinned as I closed the distance, a faint glimmer of hope blooming inside me.

I hit the bank, literally. In the white on white world I just didn't see it and walked straight into the head high, soft pile of snow that had drifted against it. Spitting snow from my mouth and wiping at my ice crystal covered face with my sleeve I searched for a way to climb up.

I hauled myself back onto land and waded through the deep snow. A small, squat, rather ugly cabin stood in front of me. I'd been sure that was what I'd seen and as I'd headed towards it I had been praying it was occupied. I know! It was never likely, I mean, if a plane crashed on your doorstep you'd come and check it out right? But I'd hoped because it had been nice to, if only for a few moments. I could see now that it definitely was not occupied, snow was drifted halfway up its windows and high against its door.

The door, when I tried it, was locked. The windows had small panes; I couldn't fit through them but one of the girls probably could. We were stuck here indefinitely; it would be sensible to get out of the plane and into the cabin. It'd be warmer, we could light a fire here which we couldn't do in the plane without the possibility of the whole thing blowing up.

Chapter 9

"We can use their telephone," was Sasha's ecstatic response to my news of a cabin.

I felt awful denting her optimism. "There's no landline I'm afraid," I said as gently as I could, "we're way too far out for that, but we'll be more comfortable in the cabin than here, warmer, we can light a fire. Will you come with me to check it out?"

The Fallons and I slithered and slipped our way back across the lake, scrambled up the bank and wallowed through the thick powdery drifts to the cabin.

"It looks like the home of a fairy-tale woodsman," said Libby

"Or," Sasha replied nervously, hanging back, "Hansel and Gretel's witch."

Sasha refused to go through the window, but Libby agreed. Just shows, you never can tell, I thought. With her outgoing nature, I'd wrongly assumed Sasha would be the braver of the two.

We broke a pane and removed the sharp shards of glass before hoisting Libby through, there was a rather worrying thud as she hit the floor on the other side. "Ow," she yelped, then, "I'm okay, I'm fine."

We walked to the door, through it we could hear Libby chattering away and thumping around but we couldn't make out her words. I looked at Emmi & raised my eyebrows in irritation. "Lib," Emmi called, "we can't hear what you're saying, and we need to come in too, could you please open the door for us?"

There was a rusty, grating sound as a key turned in the lock. Libby opened the door and the banked snow tumbled in, we clambered over the remaining pile and entered. Stepping in the doorway was like walking through a portal into a past world. There was an ancient range surrounding a large fireplace, a cracked, stained sink with a shelf above on which two battered saucepans and a few dented tin mugs and plates were stored, a threadbare sofa, a wood-wormed table and a rickety, rusted bunk bed. The air was thin and cold. The two tiny, snow covered windows let in little light, it was dark, dank and musty. Dust danced in the weak light from the open doorway and cobwebs trembled in the breeze. There was an old oil lamp together with a canister of oil and a box of matches but nothing else that would be of any use to us. There was no electricity or running water, no blankets, pillows or food. The place had either been cleared out for the winter or was a bunk house for the self-sufficient traveller.

There was a second key hanging on grimy string by the door, as dirty and rusted as the other. It opened the door to a tumbledown shed behind the cabin. In here was a small boat - a canoe I suppose - with paddles, a few old-fashioned fishing rods, a couple of canisters of what looked like petrol, two bottles of oil, a selection of water carriers, a tarpaulin, a few of lengths of rope, a saw and wooden sawhorse, a brush and shovel, an axe and a box of assorted tools.

Emmi moved thoughtfully towards the boat, I could see her mind working, knew what she was thinking because I was pondering the same thing.

"We could drag Jim here in this," she said, "and perhaps Luke. It'll be like a sledge."

We lugged the canoe out of the shed, looped one of the long, dirty rope twice and attached it to the bow. The boat, when we pulled it, skimmed nicely over the top of the snow and was easy to drag over the icy lake.

"Can we ride in it? asked Sasha. "Please, please, please!" The girls climbed in. "We're sailors on a rough sea," she pretended, they rowed with imaginary oars.

"Chased by a shark," added Libby. They rowed faster. "Santa Claus in his sleigh," Libby changed the game and they flapped imaginary reins and yelled, "faster Rudolph, faster."

"Bobsleigh riders, whooshing down a luge," yelled Sasha. Both girls hurled themselves from side to side, as fictitious corners flung them to and fro.

"Big, heavy girls with fully functioning legs," came back Emmi. "Out, you're getting hard to pull."

"Not going in it," said Luke when we arrived back at the plane, he was majorly sulky that I wasn't following any of his plans. This seemed to have stoked his inexplicable anger. His wrath was now almost palpable, I dreaded speaking to him - peace felt very fragile and my nerves were jangling. "I'll walk, it'll do me no more harm than bumping along in that thing."

He had a point. Emmi and I padded out the

canoe as best we could with an array of clothing. Then we manoeuvred Jim's deadweight out of the tiny cockpit. I took his head, Emmi his legs, we strained and staggered and with great difficulty, half carried, half dragged him as gently as we could, which actually wasn't very gently at all, out of the narrow door and into the boat.

Harvey and I eased the canoe down the bank onto the lake. Sasha launched herself in a feet first leap off the top of the bank, whooshed down on her bottom and shot out onto the frozen surface. "When we get to the cabin I'm I going to get a rod and come back out and catch us a fish from under the ice like an Eskimo," she declared. "Emmi, you can cook it for our dinner. Libby, you can help me catch it and help Emmi cook."

Libby raised her eyebrows at me, and I grinned, the two of them reminded me very much of Luke and myself.

Our journey to the cabin was slow and fraught. Luke walked slowly, deliberately, head down, completely engrossed in his own private painful struggle. It tore me apart to witness just how tough every step was for him. Sweat quickly plastered his hair to his forehead at the front of his hat and his breath was loud and ragged. His eyes, when he turned them on me, swam with agony but he picked up an awkward, uneven rhythm and just kept moving doggedly onwards.

Though Harvey and I pulled the canoe as smoothly as we could, it lurched from time to time and Jim slipped to one side or the other. Emmi trotted alongside the boat, grabbing him as he tipped but several times we had to stop for me to help her right him before moving on again. As we neared the bank it occurred to me we had not considered how we would get Jim up.

"Build a snow ramp," suggested Libby at last after much debate. It seemed a better solution than 'tying Jim in the boat with the other rope and pulling the boat up the bank,' – Sasha; or 'getting him out of the boat and dragging him to the top,' – Emmi.

So, having helped Luke up and settled him, grey faced, nauseous and sweating on the sofa in the cabin, that's what we did. The five of us sat slightly back from the top of the bank and kicked and banged our feet until the overhanging snow fell, then we formed it into the beginnings of a ramp, supplementing it with shovelfuls or bucketfuls of soft, easy to move snow from nearby drifts.

By the time we deposited Jim on the sofa beside Luke, we were rosy cheeked and panting. Luke still looked so dreadful that I passed him another couple of painkillers, even though I knew he'd taken two just before we left the plane. Sasha and Libby disappeared, returning with jubilant smiles and handfuls of icicles, as thick as their forearms and almost as long. We sucked and crunched on some of them thirstily, wincing as the sharp cold made our teeth ache. The others we crushed and wrapped in a t-shirt to make a cool pack for Luke.

We hacked at the tarpaulin in the shed with a saw, cutting a piece roughly the size of the window, then nailed it over the broken pane to stem the draught a little. Leaving Luke and Jim in the cabin, we made a return journey to the plane to bring extra clothes, a pile of the branches we'd collected and our food supply. It was mid-afternoon and the day that had never really got light was beginning to darken again. Whilst Emmi and I collected everything together, Harvey and the girls picked a spot and hacked at the ice on the lake to make a hole for Sasha to fish. "Too late today," she declared, "I'll get right on to it first thing in the morning, when the rescuers get here we can all have a lovely fish lunch together before we leave." Before we left the plane, I nipped back on board and grabbed the aircraft operating manuals – the pilot handbooks - hiding them from the others inside my coat.

Back at the time-warp cabin, after much smoking and fizzling of fir cones and needles, we persuaded the soggy, overly fresh wood to burn. We pushed one end of the sofa away from the fire so that Jim didn't get too warm, the other towards it so Luke didn't get cold. Then placed two of the water carriers, which we'd filled with ice, by the fire to melt. Snow would have been easier to put in the carriers, but Harvey informed us that snow was full of air so would melt away to very little.

"Earl Grey tea anyone," asked Emmi, waving the box and waggling a saucepan. Everyone, except Harvey, who apparently flatly refused to try new things, nodded cautiously. None of us had ever had it before or felt any enthusiasm for doing so but a hot drink did sound nice and the alternative – a cup of hot beef Oxo stock sounded very much worse.

We had our tea with crumpets we speared with twigs and toasted over the fire. They were chewy and bland when not smothered with dripping butter but hot food, nonetheless. After we'd shared the bar of chocolate for desert, we wrestled with the oil lamp, lighting it after many tries and much cursing. Then we deliberated sleeping arrangements.

"We can make you a cubbyhole on the bottom bunk Harvey," suggested Emmi.

"Luke should have the bottom bunk," I argued, "he's badly hurt, Harvey's not."

"I know," Emmi was really apologetic, making me feel guilty I'd said anything. "But if Harvey doesn't get a space of his own he'll pace and fret all night, none of us will get any rest."

So, we made Harvey a 'separate room,' on the bottom bunk by taking down the curtains from the windows and draping them over the base of the top bunk. Luke said he'd rather stay sitting on the bottom of the sofa beside his dad than try to haul his battered body up to the top bunk. So, it was decided that the girls would sleep up there together, leaving Emmi and I with the dusty floor in front of the fire.

"Can you girls go and get some more icicles to make another ice pack for Luke before bed?" asked Emmi. "Take the torch." Sasha and Libby pulled on their coats, boots and gloves and disappeared outside. Ten minutes later they still hadn't returned.

"They'll be playing," replied Emmi when I asked if we should be worried. "They'll have completely forgotten what I sent them out to do." Sure enough, the twins bounded through the door empty handed soon afterwards, singing loudly. "Icicles," reminded Emmi. Sasha and Libby turned as one, retracing their steps out of the cabin, never missing a beat. Emmi raised her palms in a 'what can you do?' gesture. I grinned.

At 6.30pm it was pitch black outside and everyone was tired, no one had slept very soundly the previous night. Emmi insisted Harvey and her sisters brush their teeth and the four of them stood side by side, shivering at the sink. "My teeth are chattering so hard I don't even need to move the brush," grumbled Sasha.

Harvey called goodnight and crawled behind his curtains with the torch from the plane. The twins climbed onto the top bunk and I hefted Malty over the rail to join them. There had been a curtain pulled aside on a wire behind the door too, Emmi had taken it down and she now used it to cover the girls and the dog. "Snug as bugs in a rug," she smiled, tucking the grimy, moth eaten fabric around the three of them.

"There are bugs in our rug," shrieked Sasha, hurling the make-shift blanket and almost poor Malty too, from the bunk, recoiling in horror. Sure enough, as the curtain hit the floor, a small family of spiders scuttled out. Deep shudders ran through both twin's small bodies as they hung over the edge of the bed, watching the hapless, scattering creatures with disgust.

"You're not scared of spiders are you Sasha? I asked with a grin.

"I'm not scared of anything," she replied,

dragging her horrified eyes from the spiders, "but can you give our blanket a really good shake outside Emmi please?"

Once Harvey and the girls were settled and we'd covered Luke and Jim with some spare clothing, Emmi beckoned me outside. I was glad to get away from Luke's black, simmering fury. The effort of patience for me was as wearing as the struggle for control for him, the tension crackled between us. I was hurt and bemused by his wrath, of course he was in pain and would be upset and scared for his dad, but it was more than that, there was something I was missing.

Emmi and I leant against the snow crusted porch railing, looking out into the night. Neither of us spoke. The silence freaked me out and I trawled my brain, seeking something, anything to say. Emmi meanwhile was calm, serene, clearly one of those unfathomably self-possessed people with absolutely no fear of silence.

"It's really quiet," I said finally.

"And dark," she replied.

"So dark," I agreed.

A tiny sliver of silver moon had appeared very briefly from behind the still thick clouds, it's curved bottom seeming to perch on the briefly illuminated mountain tops. Otherwise it was pitch black, an absolute darkness that I was pretty sure I'd never experienced at home – even cocooned in the depths of the Lake District with Mum and Colin. It was also so quiet that the very noiselessness seemed to whistle in my ears. I'd never noticed how noisy normal life was - 'we chased this kind of silence from our hectic world long, long ago,' I thought in wonder.

"Libby has enough insulin for three more days," Emmi said at last. "Jim probably can't even last that long without water and who knows what kind of danger Luke's in with those ribs. We really need the weather to change so that that search party can get its ass here and rescue us."

I almost voiced my half-formed plan. It would be good to run it past someone, say it out loud, see if it sounded even vaguely plausible, but I imagined her saying 'are you mad?' and swallowed my words at the last moment. I needed to get my thoughts in order first.

"Let's pray the cloud lifts overnight," I said instead.

I couldn't see her, but I thought she stiffened in annoyance beside me, she blew through her nose, "do you?" she began, "can you?"

"Do I, can I what?" I prompted. I had the unnerving impression she was reading my mind, was frustrated that I was holding back on her.

"Nothing," she said opening the cabin door. "Let's go and get some sleep, see what the morning brings."

Chapter 10

Five minutes later, we were bunked down under a heap of clothing on the dirty floor. I lay on my back, sleepless once again. I listened to a pair of owls having a loud, hooting conversation with one another. Earlier there'd been what I guessed to be coyotes too, their yip yapping carrying eerily in the still night air.

When I was sure everyone else was asleep, I levered myself up and crept to a pile of spare clothes, under them lay the manuals from the plane. I tiptoed back to the fire and examined them in the faint, orange light. For a person that knew how to fly a plane, these manuals contained all the information needed to pilot this particular aircraft. The sequences for powering up, starting and configuring the Otter were all there. Take-off, stall and landing speeds were listed, as was the speed data for extending or retracting the flaps. I trawled backwards and forwards through the data for a couple of hours until my eyes hurt, and my brain protested.

Hmmm, okay, back to that plan I'd begun to

cook up – the plane was, as far as I could tell at first glance, largely undamaged. There were two bottles of oil in the shed and there should be a bottle in the spares compartment in the tail section of the plane. Top up the small amount still in the engine and I reckoned we'd have perhaps seventeen litres, less than half what you'd normally take-off with but enough for a short journey. The lake, directly in front of the plane was long and flat. What if I were to refit the oil filter and replenish the oil, use the lake as a runway and fly us out of here? I was pretty sure I was capable of it. Okay, so I couldn't fly in this weather any more than a rescue plane could, but when the weather changed, which it surely must at some point, I could get us straight up and out. We'd not be relying on the searchers locating us in any brief flying window there might be.

All night long I tossed and turned, thoughts tumbling in my mind. I kept staring over at Jim, illuminated in the firelight, as if by some supernatural means he could help me with my decision, tell me I was making the right choice. I seriously did not like this decision-making stuff! I was so desperate to avoid it I was pathetically seeking the telepathic opinion of a comatose man. I allowed myself a small, self-depreciating chuckle – what next, would I be setting up a séance to commune with my dead Grandma – get her thoughts on the matter? 'Come on Nate,' I berated myself, 'stop being so lame, you're going to have to make decisions at some point in your life, now would be a really good time to start.'

But jeez, could I not have started with something smaller, something less life or death, or possibly death or death. Stay here and potentially watch three of our group die or try to fly us out and maybe kill us all – that was some monumental decision! I swung back and forth between black defeatism and giddy optimism. Both states of mind were more than a little worrying!

'Get a grip, focus, sort your head out and make a choice,' I ordered myself, muttering quietly.

As I stared at Jim my eye was caught by a small movement from Luke at the end of the sofa. He'd been so still I'd thought he was sleeping soundly but, though his eyes were closed, tears glinted on his cheeks –

pouring out of him in a silent stream of pain or sorrow, perhaps both. I debated getting up, going over to him but I knew there was nothing I could do to ease his suffering, or offer him comfort. All I could do was try to get him and his father out of here before we lost them and that was what I resolved to do.

Decision made I fell into an uneasy sleep. I must have slept for no more than a couple of hours and was woolly headed and groggy when I woke. The fire was not quite out so, cold and stiff, I pushed my icy feet into my snow boots and staggered over to add some more wood from our depleted pile. Wriggling myself as close to the fire as I could without actually sitting in the flames I sat thawing out for a few moments before heading to the window. If it was clear I'd give it today to see if anyone found us, if not I'd float my plan with everyone when they woke.

Praying for clear skies, I wiped the condensation, some of it iced, off the window, pushed myself onto my tiptoes and squeezed my face against the grimy glass to peer out past the snow heaped on the ledge. Snow tumbled down thickly and in the feeble light of dawn, I could see the clouds still heavily suffocating the land. For a moment I felt weirdly claustrophobic, I had the spooky notion that we'd been pulled from the sky into some giant snowdome, that we were the prisoners of some alien race. I imagined a sunlit world around us that we would never see again.

"Any better?" enquired Emmi, coming up behind me, making me jump again and bang my already swollen nose on the wood separating the panes.

"You've got to stop doing that," I complained, cradling my nose.

"Sorry, I'll stomp up to you tomorrow morning. If we're still here tomorrow morning that is. How is it out there?"

I shook my head, "not good." 'Get it over with,' I told myself and before I could change my mind, "I have a proposal."

I was all set to blurt my plan out. In fact, I felt so full of the words I thought they'd burst from me when I opened my mouth but at just that moment Luke began scrabbling round on the sofa, searching for his painkillers. Emmi turned and went to help him, then

Harvey's impressively tousled head appeared through his curtains. Soon the twins were up too and Malty needed to be let out and Jim's temperature had to be assessed and debated and raised with more clothing. Water needed to be boiled and everyone wanted something to eat. Harvey had eaten his own supply of 'red food,' whatever that might have been and was now slopping jam onto biscuits to make them red enough to eat.

"The fire's nice," said Sasha, stretching like a cat, dipping Hobnobs in her lukewarm Earl Grey tea. "I bet I can empty this whole cup just by dunking, I'm not going to take a single sip, not even going to lift the mug."

I found I was too nervous to eat. I sat and watched the others, rehearsing what I'd say. Malty snuggled in beside me, resting his little head on my lap, letting me stroke his silken ears.

"What's up Nate?" Libby asked. I looked at her in surprise, how did she know to ask?

"You're not eating and Malty's moved away from the packet of Hobnobs, he must think you really need him," she explained.

I smiled; she was right, Malty had become our collective comfort blanket. I hadn't had a pet before and his kindness, patience and utter dependability amazed me. He seemed possessed of an innate ability to gauge which one of us needed him most and would sidle over and lie down beside us or climb quietly on our lap so we could stroke his soft belly or wind our fingers through his short, wiry hair, he never wriggled or protested. Yesterday evening I'd watched Emmi scoop him up like a handbag and carry him onto the porch. They'd returned a short while later, Emmi with red, puffy eyes, Malty with a slightly damp coat. He appeared to consider it his function to absorb our pain and fears.

Oh well, here goes! "Okay," I said, taking a deep breath, "so Jim and Luke are pretty ill and really need to go to hospital and Lib…," I cut off at Emmi's frantic head shake. "And it may take too…" again Emmi's look of horror. "It could take a long time for a search party to find us."

"Are Luke and Mr Carter going to die?" butted

in Sasha, absentmindedly playing with Malty, flapping her fingers at the dog's mouth then pulling them away quickly as Malty snapped good naturedly at them. "If they do, will we have to eat them? I heard about people that ate other people after their plane crashed in the mountains. It's just, I don't think I could - eat them."

"Well I certainly couldn't," declared Harvey, "I don't eat meat, so I'd starve and die too but you couldn't eat me – I'm refusing permission for you to do that right now," he stabbed his finger at each of us in turn, staring threateningly.

"Well, perhaps Mr Carter," continued Sasha, "I could maybe eat him if I was really, really hungry. I mean, I really like Mr Carter and don't want him to die but he's already asleep, he wouldn't feel anything if he died, I'd feel better eating someone if I knew they hadn't suffered. If Luke's rib burst his lung his death would be painful and nasty, I couldn't eat him after watching him go through that."

Whoa! We'd gone way off track here, the suggestion I was about to make sounded completely rational and reasonable compared to this.

"No one's going to die and no one's going to be eaten," said Emmi. "Sorry," she muttered to Luke who just shrugged.

"That's right," I dived in, seizing the conversation again whilst I had the chance, "because I think I can get the plane ready to leave as soon as there is a break in the weather. I'm fairly certain the crash was caused by the oil filter working lose during the flight. I think the engineer may not have torqued it tight." I sucked in a breath and tried to slow my gabbling explanation." He was fitting a new filter when I went out to the plane with Jim, then he got a phone call, after that I never saw him go back to tighten it. I guess the turbulence we hit was enough to joggle it lose." Only Emmi appeared to be listening to me, I continued anyway. "The filter is just lying in the engine compartment, all I'd need to do would be refit it and top up the oil – there's some in the shed and there'll be a bottle in the spares compartment in the tail of the plane."

"Done it!" cheered a gleeful Sasha, cutting through my monologue. Everyone looked at her uncomprehendingly. "Emptied it. Ta dah," she proudly waved her cup upside down. It was drained of all tea but smeared with mushed biscuit. "Without a single sip." She stood and performed a theatrical bow.

"Nice one," replied Luke with genuine admiration. He gave her an awkward, wrong handed high five then turned to me, looking confused and confrontational. "Whilst it's mildly interesting to know what caused us to crash," he drawled, "why would you bother to repair the plane, my dad's not exactly in a position to fly us out of here is he?"

"No," I replied hesitating, "but he could come round at any time, right Harvey?"

Harvey nodded. "Or," I continued, taking a deep breath... just say it, just say it .... "if Jim doesn't regain consciousness I think I could fly the plane. I've learned so much from your dad - he teaches me about all aspects of flying whilst we work on the kit plane and you know how much I've played on my simulator, loads and loads. I'm pretty sure I could get us out of here."

Now I had everyone's attention. There was a

stunned silence, the others gawped at me, brows furrowed as though they were trying to solve a particularly nasty maths problem. "Bad idea, bad idea," bawled Harvey eventually, clapping his hands over his ears, clearly unable to listen anymore.

"What he said," Luke sneered, cocking his head at Harvey. "You're crazy Ellis. That's some colossal ego. I mean, who do you think you are, our great saviour, our hero?"

I shook my head furiously; my nerves were twanging enough for me to be roused very quickly to anger myself. "Ego," I hissed back, "how could I, Luke's friend Nate, possibly have an ego, I've lived my entire life in your shadow. I'm reminded every single day that I'm nothing compared to you."

"Thumper," yelled Harvey, scuttling to his bunk, hands still clasped on ears, disappearing, behind his curtain.

I was completely non-plussed, the combination of the vicious attack from my so-called-friend and Harvey yelling a seemingly random word before dashing to his bunk like a tortoise diving into its shell, confused me no-end.

I turned to Emmi, raising my eyebrows and palms, pleading for explanation. "From Bambi, you know, Thumper the rabbit," she said.

Well now I'd gone from bewildered to confounded, had everyone gone mad?

"If you can't say something nice, don't say nothing at all," Libby elucidated. "Our Mum says it to us all the time."

"Ahh," I smiled, feeling my fury melt. Even Luke gave a little chortle, seemed to shake himself up a bit.

"What's wrong with you Luke?" asked Emmi hesitantly, bravely though. My tactic would have been to move on, ignore him and hope he'd sort himself out.

I watched him, half fascinated, half appalled. I saw him grapple for control, lose. Watched his anger swell up and spill out of him. "Wrong?" he hissed furiously, clutching his side as the force of his words yanked at his broken ribs. "Wrong," he repeated, struggling for breath, "what on earth could possibly be wrong? I mean obviously it's completely fine that I'm in agony and sat here hour after hour, staring at my dad, waiting and watching for his next breath whilst you chase after 'Captain Save the Day,' he cocked his head at me contemptuously. "For God's sake, why doesn't someone back me up and just tell him he's a disillusioned fool to think he can fly us out of here."

"You are just a kid Nate," Sasha said in a small voice. "Kids can't fly planes, if Mr Carter crashed and he's an adult and a proper pilot and everything, then there's no way you won't crash too!"

I shook my head, "Jim didn't crash, it was unsafe to continue to fly without oil to cool the engine, it would have overheated and seized, and we'd have gone into a stall and dropped out of the sky – crashed for real. He did the only thing he could do - shut down the engine and glide us in as carefully as he could. If he could have seen enough to avoid the trees he'd probably have got us down without a scratch."

"So, it wasn't Dad's fault? Luke asked incredulously, his eyes wide.

"No," finally I understood Luke's fury and distress. "No Luke, your dad did everything right. It wasn't his fault we came down, in fact it's due to his brilliant flying that we're all still alive, not bodies dangling in mangled wreckage from trees.

The black mood that had hung on Luke since the crash lifted, I could almost see it waft up and away like foul, sinister smoke. He touched Jim's hand tenderly and a tear dribbled down his cheek.

No one quite knew what to do or say so we all just stared awkwardly at our feet. "Harvey," Luke called at last in a slightly wavering voice, "you're safe to come out of your hidey hole now, Mr Hyde has left the building, Dr Jekyll is back in residence."

Everyone giggled, I put my hand on his knee and he covered it briefly with his own. "Sorry mate," he said.

"S'no problem. Look," I steered us back on topic, "under different circumstances I wouldn't suggest piloting the plane myself, but I've spent the night weighing up our options and, ridiculous as it sounds, I honestly think it might be the best possibility for getting us all out of here alive. Of course, we could just sit tight and wait for rescue, but we have no idea how long it might take anyone to find us. We're a long way off our intended route and literally in the middle of nowhere." Harvey slouched back to the group and patted Luke roughly on his good shoulder. "Our ELT will stop transmitting sometime today, it only has about fifty hours of battery life, but even if it were to continue someone would need to be flying practically overhead to detect the signal. Unless they've narrowed the search to the right area, there's slim chance of that, we're nowhere near a regular flight path."

"Jim and Luke both need urgent hospitalisation and we need to get to a doctor for more….," Emmi's eyes widened again, "for other reasons," I finished lamely. "The rest of you don't have to come with me, everyone will have to make up their own mind. I could just fly out and give the search team our location. Just remember though, that with the weather the way it is, there's no guarantee that they'd be able to get back in to rescue you."

I fully expected them to reiterate that I was mad, to reject the idea completely but they didn't. Everyone was silent, weighing up our situation in their own mind, concluding it was dire enough to warrant desperate measures. Emmi spoke first, "Do you really believe you can take off and fly that plane and land us safely?" she asked.

I looked at them, at their worried, hopeful faces. I knew what they needed me to say so I swallowed my own huge, banging doubts and conjured up a positive smile, taking time to make sure my tone held the sharp briskness of confidence. "I do," I nodded, "I've studied the plane's manuals and gone over every bit of the flight in my mind - the procedures I'd need to follow, the things I'd need to do. I've mentally done the whole thing – got us up, flown us out and got us down again. I really believe I know enough to do it." I was surprised at how sure I managed to sound - during the long night I'd silently argued the exact opposite with just as much conviction but no one else needed to know that did they?!

"Okay then," Emmi replied. "I think we should all come with you." I looked at Luke, he shrugged. I flopped back against the sofa. I suddenly had the weak, washed out kind of feeling you get after you've been up all night with a nasty vomiting bug. There had been way too many emotions, too many huge issues to deal with in too short a time. "If Mr Bean can do it then why can't Nate?" asked Emmi. "Rowan Atkinson," she continued as we all looked at her uncomprehendingly, "took the controls of a plane over Kenya when his pilot passed out."

"Really?" I asked. Feeling a little buoyed.

"Absolutely," she replied. "Though he didn't have to take off and the pilot came round before they had to land."

Right!!

"But Nate, we absolutely can't leave until I've caught a fish," declared Sasha and everyone laughed, breaking the tension.

Chapter 11

After banking the fire for Luke, the Fallons and I donned extra layers, preparing to head back to the plane. Emmi caught me staring as she dressed the twins. "What?" she asked.

"I'm just wondering if you're ever going to stop," I replied, nodding at the twins who'd been transformed into fat cartoon figures – Teletubbies - almost as wide as they were tall in their huge volume of clothing.

"It's cold out there" she grinned, squeezing a placidly waiting Libby into her coat, squashing her jumpers down with one hand, tugging at the gaping zip with the other. She wriggled and shrugged herself into her own coat and pulled a hat on her head. The plaid hat had side flaps that hung down like the floppy ears of a spaniel – she looked ridiculous. Ridiculous and, I blushed just thinking it, a tiny bit cute, black eyes and swollen nose notwithstanding.

We waddled out of the door. She was right, it was cold, seriously, brutally cold and there was a biting wind, several degrees and a good few knots the wrong side of bracing. I looked around our white world, it was empty and wild, formidably bleak and staggeringly beautiful in equal measure.

The Fallons and Malty romped merrily in the snow. I grinned, I loved how into each other they were, they really seemed to enjoy each other's company, sure they bickered, I supposed like any other siblings, but it was always good natured. It did my heart good to watch them frolicking like they hadn't a care in the world. You had to admire the indomitably buoyant nature of the human spirit. How good we were at making fun and finding joy, even in the most desperate of circumstances.

In the shed, Emmi and I rooted through the jumbled toolbox. When Colin had tightened the oil filter on the car he'd used a wrench, the box seemed to contain every tool known to man except – you've got it – a wrench! I raised my palms and eyebrows, scowling in defeat at Emmi.

"No," she said determinedly, "we're not falling at the first hurdle." She rooted through the box again, lifted some tools, stared at them then discarded them with a small shake of her head. She picked up a socket extension handle and turned it over in her hand a few times, deep in thought.

"I don't see how….," I began, but she held up her hand to shush me and disappeared out of the shed. She returned a few moments later carrying one of the tin mugs and a large handkerchief.

"Watch," she said. She formed the handkerchief into a circle and tied a lose knot. Waved the socket extension in the air, like a magician about to perform an elaborate trick, then held it against the knot and, with a flourish, tied a second knot over it. She put the circle over the mug and began to twist the extension handle.

I grinned, and nodded, impressed. The leverage allowed her to tighten the handkerchief evenly and firmly round the mug. "Grips really well," she said, clearly pleased with herself, "we'll be able to tighten the filter perfectly with that." She gave a small bow and handed me the bits of improvised torque.

I pushed them, together with a fairly random selection of other tools in my rucksack and grabbed the two oil canisters. Then we went back outside to collect Harvey and the girls from where they still gambolled about, careering round with happy abandon, Malty floundering after them as best as his short legs would allow.

"Need a rod," was Sasha's response when Emmi told them it was time to go. She dashed to the shed. I followed her back, I'd had a thought, I picked up a paddle. Emmi raised her eyebrows when she saw me with it.

"Wait and see," I said, she wasn't the only one that could improvise tools.

"Let's play I Spy," suggested Sasha, as we trekked back through the newly fallen snow, slithered down the bank to the lake and walked to the plane.

"I spy with my little eye, something beginning with S," boomed Harvey. How can someone that can't tolerate noise speak in such a loud voice all the time, I marvelled?!!

"Snow," yelled the girls in unison.

"Correct." We all howled with laughter.

"Snow is falling," bellowed Harvey, in a flat,

entirely tune-free, drone. "All around me."

"Children playing, having fun," joined in the girls.

"Tis the season, love and understanding," I added my voice to theirs, though I was pretty sure I hadn't sung out loud since nursery. "Merry Christmas, everyone." Because it was the only bit of the song we knew we sang it over and over, really belting it out, our voices stuttering with laughter. It felt great, perfect, though it was long past Christmas and as far removed from a merry time as any could be.

We couldn't see the plane until we were almost on top of it. The clouds continued to lie weightily on the land, I tried to spot the join but there was no end to the earth, no beginning to the sky, just a great blurry, yellowy grey bubble in which we were trapped. "It's like all colour's been drained from the world isn't it?" observed Libby, giving a little shiver.

Emmi and I left Harvey and the girls at the edge of the lake, just below the plane. Harvey said he would help the girls batter back through the layer of ice that had already formed over the fishing hole they'd made yesterday. "Won't the fuel have frozen in these temperature's too?" asked Emmi.

I shook my head, "it's AVGas which has a freezing point of minus fifty-eight degrees Celsius, it'll be fine. We've got plenty," I added, "extra in the reserve tank if we need it. Enough for me to make a complete hash of landing at Old Crow and be able to go-round several times."

As I had expected, the plane was covered in icy snow, the cowling frozen shut, glistening fringes of icicles hanging from its underside. I turned to Emmi and brandished the paddle with the same level of showmanship she had employed in the shed, then used it scrape off the icy covering of snow. It made a perfect scraper, was strong and wide, plastic so it didn't stick and smooth enough not to damage the metal. Once the snow was cleared I unfastened the clips then wriggled a large flat blade screwdriver under the flap until it opened. I lifted out the oil filter.

"One all," conceded Emmi." I turned the filter over in my hand, examining it carefully, it was entirely undamaged.

"It's fine," I cleaned it off and screwed it back on.

"Don't we need to fill it first?" asked Emmi.

I shook my head. "The oil top up pipe is on the fuselage, just below the door."

"Right." She performed her trick with the torque.

Harvey had re-joined us, "nice one Emmi," he hollered.

I tested it and nodded in agreement, "tight as can be, can't budge it at all. Harvey, can you grab the canisters from the canoe, I'll get the bottle of oil from the spares box and we'll get it topped up."

"There'll not be enough," Harvey said. "An Otter needs about thirty-six litres in it at take-off, we'll have nowhere near that."

"I know," I agreed. "I reckon there'll be about five litres left in the engine. We've got ten in the canoe, I'm hoping there will be two more in the spares box. At seventeen litres we'll have less than half of what we should have."

I thought Harvey would just say we should

forget the whole thing, he wasn't exactly a risk taker and he thought the whole thing was a bad idea anyway, but he surprised me. "Hmm," he pondered. "I guess we've not got far to fly to Old Crow, you could probably get away with it Nate if you don't fly at full power."

That was my opinion too. "It'll help that the engine's cool to begin with and we'll be flying through really cold air, that will hopefully stop the engine getting too hot."

Harvey nodded, "yep, should be okay, you'll need to keep an eye on it though or you'll end up having to shut down the engine like Mr Carter did. You won't make such a good job of gliding us down though, with you at the controls we'd be certain to crash for real if we lost the engine."

"Yeah, thanks for pointing that out Harvey."

"S'no problem," replied Harvey, missing my sarcasm completely. He headed for the canoe to fetch the canisters.

Emmi and I trooped to the back of the plane. The spare kit would be stored in the tail, we could have got to it from inside, but I knew there'd be an access hatch on the outside too. I was surprised to find the hatches' catch unhooked. I pulled it open …. empty!

"You have got to be kidding," I yelled upwards, cursing the cosmic conspirators that were most certainly having a good laugh at our expense from on high.

"How can it be empty?" asked Emmi.

I shrugged, "I suppose one of the branches must have snagged the hook and everything must have fallen out as we came down."

"Can we use the oil that's in the cabin?" she asked, "you know, the stuff for the lamp."

I shook my head, "it's kerosene, not oil, different thing altogether."

Emmi was silent for a few minutes, "right then," she finally declared, her voice cheery - did the girl never lose her temper, or her optimism? "The spare bottle can't be far if we lost it after we first hit the trees, right? I know we didn't see it yesterday but if we follow back further along the edge of the forest we should come across it shouldn't we?"

144

"Possibly," it was worth a try. It had snowed a fair bit since we'd come down but there was a chance the bottle wouldn't be completely obscured.

"I'll just tell the girls where we're going, see if they want to come," Emmi said, heading down to the lake. A few moments later she returned alone, the twins were fully immersed in their fishing and didn't want to join our expedition.

"Okay team," I said, "eyes down, let's find that bottle of oil." The three of us set off, splitting up, walking parallel to each other a short distance apart, Harvey at the tree line, Emmi and I slightly farther into the forest.

After a short while Harvey yelled, "I've not found the oil," he boomed as we reached him, "but it might not be worth searching for it anyway, look at this."

On the ground at his feet, partially submerged in new snow, lay a chunk of black rubber, a short way away lay another and another – rubber and smashed plastic that looked suspiciously like shredded tyre and broken ski. "Is it ours?"

145

"Unless another plane has come down in the last few days in the same place, I reckon it is," I answered sarcastically. I was gutted, I knew it would be the tail wheel and ski. I hadn't noticed that it was damaged when I'd checked the plane yesterday, the snow must have drifted under the tail, hiding it. With hindsight, I knew I should have looked more closely, there'd been that great ripping metal sound as we'd come down, that huge jar as we'd hit something hard with the back end of the plane. I'd been too ready to think the plane was still useable.

The sepia, heavy, low pressing clouds suddenly felt even more menacing. I'd thought we were going to triumph, but it seemed that this inhospitable land had got the better of us after all. I cackled manically, startling myself with the sound that was somewhere between a laugh and a howl. "You win," I yelled at the gloom above.

"Jeez," I chortled turning to the Emmi, who was regarding me warily, "when the universe is trying to tell you something it really doesn't mess about does it!" Harvey had his hands clapped over his ears again to drown out my yelling.

"Can't we fly without a tyre?" she asked.

"We could certainly fly without it, probably even land but I wouldn't risk taking off on a bare wheel," I answered, completely deflated. "There's no way we can leave here without it."

"No," agreed Harvey, "especially not since we'll have to take-off over the lake which won't be smooth. Hit one rut without a tyre and we'd be in trouble."

I nodded, "ground looping,"

"Ground looping," confirmed Harvey.

"English?" demanded Emmi.

"Sorry, ground looping is where a tail dragger, which is what our Otter is, loses directional control, which it could if we hit a rut without a tyre to cushion the impact. It pulls itself into a tight loop, which a pilot can't steer out of, then becomes unstable. If the plane tilts, the wing will hit the ice, rip the tip then we'd be going nowhere."

"Right," affirmed Harvey.

"Right," acquiesced Emmi dismally, even her

147

hopefulness finally dented. "No point in continuing our search for the spare oil canister then."

"None," I kicked in fury at the tyre pieces, fighting tears.

"I didn't think Nate should try to fly us out anyway," said Harvey cheerfully. Let's go back to the cabin, I like it here, it's peaceful, we can just stay."

"How about we do go back to the cabin, brainstorm, see if we can come up with a Plan B," placated Emmi, seeing my thunderous face.

"What, like clapping for Tinkerbell?!" I huffed, booting the rubber some more. There was no Plan B, other than to pray that someone found us before one or all of Jim, Luke and Libby died. I'd never have suggested flying the plane out of here if I could have thought of an alternative. The others would never have agreed to my plan if they could have come up with anything else themselves.

As we trudged back to the girls, I felt myself begin to give in to the pull of giving up. Slipping from being crushed by our inability to carry out my plan to being relieved we couldn't. There was something very seductive about resigning myself to the fact that our salvation was no longer in my hands – we'd either be rescued in time to save Jim, Luke, and Libby or we'd not. It was comforting to mentally shrug and say 'hey, I tried my best.'

Sasha and Libby were lying on their bellies on the icy lake, fatly padded, multi-coloured seals, heads pressed together, peering intently into their fishing hole. My sanguinity vanished; a huge lump formed in my throat as I looked at Libby. When I turned to Emmi she was staring at her sister with tears in her eyes too.

"Of course," said Harvey without preamble, "it doesn't have to have a wheel." Emmi and I looked at him puzzled. "I mean," he continued, "lots of planes around here just have skis for taking off and landing on the snow."

"Harvey," I yelled, forgetting his dislike of raised voices, startling him and making him slap his hands over his ears. "Sorry," I continued, lowering my voice, "but you're a genius."

"I know," agreed Harvey, "everyone tells me that."

"That's a fantastically brilliant suggestion." I continued, "we've got snowboards on board, if we can work out how to replace the wheel with one of those we'll probably be able to take off on it. Come on," I surged, revitalised, as fast as I was able, back through the deep snow towards the plane. "Let's go look at the wheel fitting, see if we can work out how to get it off and replace it with a snowboard."

Chapter 12

Sound clearly travelled in our cloud insulated land. "What you yelling about Nate?" enquired Sasha, wading towards us, Libby at her heels.

"Our back tyre's burst and the ski's ripped off," I explained, "but Harvey," I went to clap him on the shoulder, but he ducked smartly out of my reach, "has come up with a fabulous solution."

Crafting makeshift landing gear was an interesting enough project to tempt the twins to abandon their fishing and join us. We hadn't brought the shovel from the shed so together we kicked at the snow around the plane's tail to loosen it then scooped up armfuls, throwing it to the side, only to have most of it blow back over us in the steadily rising wind, freezing immediately on our clothes, hats and faces. White crusted we bent down together, jostling to look. The wheel was bolted to a stirrup shaped curve of metal which in turn was bolted to the plane's undercarriage. The wheel was twisted but that didn't matter, it was coming off anyway. The bolts attaching the stirrup to the wheel and the plane were fine, I was sure I could take them out and re-use them but the metal arch itself was bent and useless. "Hmm."

"More problems," sang Harvey.

"Can someone grab a snowboard from the plane?" I asked, determined not to give in to melodramatic doom and gloom so easily again. Sasha and Libby dashed off, elbowing each other to be first onto the plane and came back carrying an end of the board each.

I held the board against the metal legs and everyone's heads crowded in again as we studied it. Right," I said, "so, we can remove the bindings from the board, and I don't know …. perhaps screw a strong chock of wood into the centre." We can re-use the bolts from the wheel, but we'll need to find an arched piece of metal, like this," I touched the one on the wheel, "to screw onto the wood and bolt onto the plane. I can't think of anything off the top of my head, why don't we all scour the plane, inside and out, see if we can find anything that might work?"

"Bracket?" asked Libby.

"Yes," I replied, "something that we could use as a bracket."

"No, I mean could we use a bracket? There's one on the guttering along the eaves at the back of the cabin. The snow's banked so high around there that Sasha and I can reach the roof - the guttering's got some fantastic icicles on it - remember we brought everyone one to suck yesterday? Well, I snapped another one off to eat this morning, it was right on top of a metal bracket that looked just like that," she pointed at the metal ring.

"Hey, well done Libby," praised Emmi, patting the girl on the head as though she were a dog. "Well spotted, the bracket sounds like it will be perfect." I heard Sasha huff down her nose, she folded her arms across her chest in a strop, clearly unhappy that her sister was receiving such praise.

"Yeah," I agreed, ignoring Sasha, "a fantastic idea Libby. "Now, we've two options: we can continue our search for the oil or; take the snowboard back to the cabin, get this bracket and start work on the adaptations?"

153

Whilst we'd been studying the wheel, it had begun to snow really hard and the wind was now gusting forcefully, shrieking and howling around the plane, rocking it to and fro. Ice crystals had already pearled on our snow splattered bodies. Tiny glittering icicles clung to the tendrils of hair that had escaped our hats, even to our eyebrows and eyelashes. My fingers were beginning to scream their objection to the biting cold and the frigid air was burning at the exposed skin on my face, numbing my chin and sending sharp pains up my already sore nose with every breath.

"Head back," mumbled Sasha awkwardly through frozen lips. She stuffed Malty under her outer jacket to protect him from the worst of the weather, "please."

"Good choice Sash," agreed Harvey, turning and striding to the bank.

We staggered into the raging wind across the lake, heads down, blasted and blinded by sleet. "Hurts," gasped Sasha, "got my eyes closed, someone stop me if I go off the wrong way." I took her arm, steering her, shivering as great icy lumps slid down my neck behind my bowed head in an ever-increasing frozen river. We scrambled up the bank, surged through the deepening snow to the cabin and burst through the door, ice coated, red nosed and cheeked and blue lipped. Panting with the effort of battling the wind, stamping thick snow from our boots and banging our crusty white gloved hands together.

"We've lost the spare oil, but we're gonna find it and the tail wheel's all broken but we're gonna fix it," Sasha gabbled at Luke, determined to be the centre of attention again.

"Well whoop-de-do," was Luke's snide reply. We all snapped our heads to him in surprise, I thought we'd moved on from his bad mood, Sasha looked like she might cry. Though it was physically warmer inside, the atmosphere was positively arctic. Luke's contempt seemed to fill the entire cabin, bounce from the walls and smack us in the face. This wasn't the tormented fury of last night, he just sounded petulant and Sasha's stroppy, jealous face when Libby came up with the bracket solution sprang into my mind. He just didn't like me being the one calling the shots.

'Well guess what Luke, you'll just have to get used to it,' I thought. 'I quite like being this new Nate.' It was true I realised suddenly, I'd started to feel quite comfortable, nice and peaceful inside. I felt…. right, I'd spent my life feeling like I was a person that was not quite me, like someone cowering inside me, now I felt whole, like I was upright inside, filling my whole body. It was good.

Chapter 13

"I don't want Earl Grey, I want hot chocolate," moaned Sasha as Libby handed her another lukewarm cup of tea, "and some real food."

Mmm, real food would be good, we'd scoffed the crumpets, crisps and Emmi's healthy snacks and were pretty much left with biscuits. I couldn't have foreseen a time when I'd object to living on chocolate digestives, but I'd gladly swap them for a piece of chicken or a bacon sandwich right now.

"How about I boil up some Oxo cubes and we dip Water Biscuits in,' suggested Emmi.

"Eeugh," Sasha wrinkled her nose.

"It'll be warm and meaty," Emmi reassured her, "just what your tummy needs."

"No, my tummy needs steak and eggs and crusty bread," Sasha disagreed, "and some cucumber," she added as an afterthought.

"Well, that's what it can have as soon as we get out of here," replied Emmi.

Which of course prompted an immediate

discussion of the first meal we would order once we made it back to civilisation – chicken and chips for me, salmon and new potatoes for Emmi, a hamburger for Luke, milky porridge and toast and jam for Libby and tomato soup for Harvey – "because it's the most colourful, cheeriest, prettiest food there is."

Once we'd finished eating, the twins led Emmi and I around the back of the cabin to show us the bracket, Sasha surging ahead so she could point it out first.

The screws were rusty, I couldn't get the screwdriver to grip them at all. Emmi fetched a hammer and I banged the screwdriver against a screw furiously. "Come on, come on," I yelled. Could nothing just be simple!!

Eventually the screwdriver caught in the groove of the first screw. "Ah ha," I declared in triumph. I had to the remove my thick outer gloves to get a good enough grip to unscrew it, I'd been about to take off my silk inner gloves too, but Emmi had stopped me.

"Don't touch any metal out here with your bare hands, it's so cold your skin could stick to it." Ouch, good point!

It took ages, there were six screws, each were stubbornly stuck. I was frustrated, impatient with my clumsiness, the poor, weak grip of my stiff, frozen fingers. The sleet had turned to beating hail and, though we were sheltered from the worst of the wind behind the cabin, it was seriously cold. The twins soon disappeared back inside. Emmi and I took turns with the screws, we didn't speak to each other but muttered and cursed constantly. As soon as we'd handed the screwdriver over, we jammed our hands awkwardly back into our ski gloves - it was difficult to force numb, unbending fingers into thick, padded gloves. We then squashed our stiff frozen hands into the pits of our arms or between our legs to try to get some warmth back into them. Alternating this with whirling our cold, heavy arms or stamping our feet, desperate to restart our sluggish circulation.

As she unscrewed the last screw Emmi cut her hand, red blood dripped through her ripped inner glove and spread on the snow. She didn't even notice, couldn't feel it, seemed surprised when I pointed it out.

Finally, the bracket fell into the snow, I reached down but found I could no longer pick it up in my useless fingers. Emmi hooked it with her toe, pushed it into my arms and we stumbled inside.

I dropped the bracket on the floor, pulled off both pairs of gloves and staggered to the fire, zombie style, holding my frozen hands in front of me.

"Don't ….," began Harvey, as I plunged them into the pan of warm water on the hearth. A searing pain burned along my fingers, so intense that it made me sick to my stomach.

"Yeeagh," I yelled, snatching them back out and jamming them between my legs, bending double as my stomach roiled. "Argh, Argh, Argh," I moaned, dancing about, my face twisted in pain.

"Slowly," bellowed Harvey, he was wearing his ear defenders, I presume because the hail was rattling on the cabin roof like dried peas in a tin. "You need to warm your fingers slowly, they're very white. They should turn red in patches as the blood begins to flow again, if they don't turn you're in trouble…. frostbite," he clarified at my questioning look.

'Marvellous.' For the next twenty minutes Emmi and I alternated between sitting on our hands and holding them out to the fire, creeping closer and closer so they weren't exposed to too much heat too quickly. The twins peered over our shoulders, watching in horrified fascination, waiting for the red to bloom and spread. Eventually our hands turned from corpse claws back into hands.

"Phew," muttered Emmi faintly. Yeah, lesson learned, we wouldn't be getting that cold again in a hurry.

"Let's have a look at that snowboard," I suggested when we'd thawed somewhat.

"Let's look at it over here," suggested Emmi, "include Luke," she whispered as I headed to the door to grab it.

As soon as she said it I knew it was a good idea to get him involved. It would not have occurred to me though, 'where does she get it from?' I wondered, impressed, 'this emotional intelligence and maturity, this ability to imagine what it would feel like to be another person.' I castigated myself for my own empathy deficit. I struggled to work myself out, I stood no chance of determining what made someone else tick!

"So," she said to Luke patting the snowboard, "the tail ski is gone, and the tyre is shredded, we've no spare tyre so the wheel is useless."

"But you could replace it with that board," said Luke, shuffling a little more upright, looking interested.

"Right," I agreed, giving Emmi a sideways smile, relieved to have my friend back on-side.

"You'll need to get the bindings off first," commanded Luke, well and truly back in the driving seat where he was comfortable and accustomed to being.

For once everything went smoothly, we found a screwdriver that fit, 'hurray,' and the screws came out quickly and smoothly, 'double hurray.'

"What next," I asked Luke. I'd already worked it out for myself, but I was working hard on the diplomacy thing.

"Hmm," Luke tilted his head, scrutinising the stripped-down board, 'you can't fit the bracket to that, you'll need to attach something to the board that you can then bolt the bracket onto."

Agreed. I waited it out silently.

"Two thick pieces of wood, one either side of the board should do it. Is there anything suitable outside?"

I opened my mouth, caught Emmi's eye, shut it again. "The porch balustrade," Luke got there at last, cut a couple of bits of that, it should be perfect."

Bingo! "Right," I said, "great idea, better get back out there before it gets dark and we can't see what we're doing." I glanced wistfully at the fire.

Emmi groaned, "sawing should at least be a warmer job than unscrewing I suppose," she said as she shrugged back into her outer clothes.

Outside the wind had dropped a bit and the hail had stopped, it was snowing again but gently. The twins decided they would come out too, to make snow animals whilst we sawed. Even Luke wrapped up and walked gingerly outside to watch the girls.

Emmi and I cleared one of the balustrades of its covering of snow and ice, then I began sawing, using the small, rusty, frustratingly blunt hand saw from the toolbox. To say it was hard going would be putting it mildly. The balustrade was thick and wet and the old saw, far from in tip top condition, kept catching so that I'd have to stop and wriggle at it until it came unstuck. Once again Emmi and I took turns, by the time we'd finished it was beginning to turn dusk and a yellow moon hung in the sky, perching again on the towering peaks of the mountains.

"Luke spelled his name in the snow with wee," Sasha informed us in awe as we joined them. "Wicked huh?, I tried to do mine but well…. it's not as easy for a girl is it?"

Emmi started, widened her eyes at Luke.

"Not in front of the girls obviously," he clarified. "Pretty good with just my left hand though, right?"

We giggled. "Wow," gasped Emmi, regarding the profusion of snow animals. "You two have been hard at work, they're fantastic."

"The mouse that I made is the best," declared Sasha, "go and have a look at his back, I've given him a super-duper long tail." Emmi looked at me, eyebrows raised into her ridiculous hat. I lifted my shoulders in a surreptitious shrug, I didn't know which one the mouse was either. There were about a dozen, indistinguishable, vaguely animal shaped lumps of snow, I scanned them frantically.

'Aha, big round ears!' I grabbed Emmi's arm and dragged her to the most mouse like heap, we peered down its back, long thin tail, phew! "It's fabulous, Sash," gushed Emmi, "really well done."

Suddenly there was a deafening, grinding, grating roar. The twins gave simultaneous terrified yelps and hurled themselves at Emmi. The door of the cabin flung open and Harvey charged out in his stockinged feet, pulling up short. In front of the porch lay an enormous heap of snow, the fire had clearly warmed the roof enough to thaw it so that it slid off in a huge, noisy avalanche.

"Going to either have to dig, or scale your way back in," yelled Harvey. "Oh, my feet are soaking and freezing," he hopped from one to the other then dashed back inside.

I looked at Luke, he wasn't going to be climbing snow hills anytime soon. "Better get digging," I said to the girls.

Chapter 14

Back inside, we drilled clumsy holes through the snowboard and chocks of wood, then attached the two, screwing the bracket to the top. It looked like a DT project that wasn't going to make the grade. Still, it would probably do the job. "Top work,' praised Sasha, peering over my shoulder.

"Why thank you kind lady," I replied, bowing from the waist.

"It should be fairly easy to remove the wheel, then fit that to the plane in the morning," I continued, "but we'll need to jack the tail up first. I think there's just enough light with that moon to go back outside, I'm going to look around to see what I can find to use as a jack."

The Fallons all came with me and we split up to search. After a short while Libby called us over, she'd walked smack-bang into a pile of snow covered, squat sections of tree trunk piled by the edge of the wood. They were obviously waiting to be chopped into logs at some point but would fulfil our needs perfectly in the meantime. Sasha discovered a solid looking wooden pole from some long since fallen down fence. The wooden sawhorse in the shed, we decided, would make a perfect support for the tail once we had it jacked up. We piled a selection of trunk rounds of differing thicknesses and the other items into the canoe, along with the board, and a heap of tools and called it a night. The day had gone well, and we were all in a jubilant, hopeful mood.

After supper - savoury biscuits, followed by sweet biscuits – followed by Kendal Mint Cake - yum, we all crashed out in front of the fire. The twins snuggled up one either side of Luke with their DVD player. "What are you three watching?" Emmi asked after a half hour or so.

"Nothing," responded Luke, shoving the girls away from him quickly.

Libby giggled but kept quiet, Sasha had no such restraint "Barbie and the Twelve Dancing Princesses," she grinned.

"Sasha," groaned Luke, blushing furiously. "Well," he defended, "I haven't got an iPad to play on,

I'm bored out of my mind. At least watching Barbie is something to do."

"Don't worry Luke," said Emmi in a serious voice, "your secret is safe. What happens in the wilderness stays in the wilderness."

I smiled at them sleepily. All of a sudden, I felt like I'd completed a mental and physical marathon and a tidal wave of weariness swamped me. The bustling, lively chatter of the others slowed, then faded into the background and I fell into a restless, dream-filled sleep.

In my dream, the seven of us were together, in a canoe, heading along a beautiful peaceful stretch of river when suddenly we turned a corner and were right in the midst of churning rapids, being swept towards a great waterfall. We started to paddle frantically but knew it was pointless, we were going over the top, there was nothing we could do about it. From nowhere, a huge, beautiful electric blue and gold bird swooped and grabbed our boat in its talons, plucking us from the water. The bird set us down gently on top of a grassy hill, but the canoe tipped, and Jim, Luke and Libby rolled out and down the slope. At the bottom of the hill a band of nasty looking goblins stood around the gaping mouth of a black cave, Jim, Luke and Libby rolled right in and the goblins leaped in after them and pushed a huge boulder over the opening before we could reach them. There was nothing we could do, Jim, Luke and Libby were lost to us.

I gasped and jolted upright, startling the others. "All right Nate?" enquired Luke.

"Sure," I managed. Emmi raised her eyebrows, I shook my head, it didn't take a genius to interpret the symbolism in that dream, no way I was going to discuss that with them.

When Luke was dozing after his latest round of painkillers and the twins were finally in bed - we'd had to shake their 'blanket,' out, then examine every inch of it before Sasha would let Emmi tuck them in - I beckoned Emmi and Harvey outside.

It had stopped snowing now, in fact, I noted with surprise, the clouds had lifted altogether, and the heavens were bright, sprinkled with brilliant, sparkling starlight. In the silence an animal called – coyote? wolf? I didn't even know what they had in this part of the world, let alone how they sounded. Regardless, the call emphasised the solitude of the inhospitable land. Reinforced the rawness and elemental wildness of the place.

"Nice," Harvey breathed, quietly for once.

"You really like it here, don't you Harv?" asked Emmi fondly.

"I do, I feel like I can really live here, not just get from one end of the clattering, jostling day to the other. It's like a holiday for my soul…. and my ears," he added after a moment.

I caught the glint of a tear in Emmi's eye, I felt fairly choked myself. I gave myself a shake, there was a reason I'd brought them out here.

"Luke's going to be out of painkillers tomorrow morning," I said, killing the warm fuzzy mood stone dead, "and Jim will have been without food and water for three days. I can't see us getting the plane sorted tomorrow in time for us to fly out of here in daylight, which means we are here for at least another day. We might get out the following morning if the weather lets us, but we can't bank on it. Is there anything else we can do for them Harvey?"

"In the case of the broken rib," he replied, impersonalising his answer, making it academic, hypothetic again, "there's nothing to be done. It would be better to continue to manage the patient's pain but if analgesics are no longer available...." he shrugged.

"A coma patient is in danger of death from dehydration after about three or four days."

"There's a syringe in the first aid kit we brought off the plane," said Emmi. "Could we dribble some water into Mr Carter's mouth from that?"

Harvey looked doubtful, "most coma patients lose their ability to swallow. They are tube fed because there is a risk of them choking if anything is given orally, or aspirating – drawing water into their lungs, which can be very dangerous."

"Oh no," I groaned, "so Jim's doomed if we don't get some water into him and doomed if we do."

"Some coma patients can swallow."

"So, should we try to give Jim water or not?" I pushed, "this hypothetical stuff is all well and good, but we need to make a real, actual decision fast."

Harvey turned abruptly and walked back into the cabin, banging the door behind him. "You know by now you just can't push him," Emmi admonished.

I sighed, "what do you think then?"

Emmi paced up and down the short porch, her thoughts driving her physically forwards.

"If he hasn't come round by tomorrow morning I say we go for it," she said at last. "Surely if we just drip in water very slowly we can't do too much damage, if it looks like Mr Carter is choking we can just stop."

"Right," I agreed. "Emmi," I began, she lifted her eyes to look at me from under the peak of her idiotic hat. 'Hmm,' I wanted to tell her how fabulous she was – how I was blown away by the fact that she was putting her trust in me, helping with everything, never questioning, just doing as I asked her. How impressed I was that she never complained at the biting agony of the cold, the difficulty of the tasks that faced us. How I could never have done it without her. "Let's call it a day," I stuttered at last.

"Right oh,' she agreed, heading back inside.

The sleep that had swallowed me up so readily, so greedily earlier, had backed right off, coiled in its grasping tentacles and scuttled away. I imagined it sitting cockily in the corner mocking me. The night was unbearably long. The windows rattled in their panes, the tarpaulin over the broken pane flapping noisily. Wind gusted under the door and howled down the chimney. I tossed and turned as the others slept as soundly as our hibernating bear neighbours. The fear demons rose and attacked me in the darkness, spearing my mind with shards of doubt. The full weight of responsibility weighed on me. The sleeping children believed in me, what if their faith was misplaced? I worried that the lake would be too short for take-off, that the ice would be too thin, that I'd crash on take-off, that I'd crash on landing, that the weather would never be good enough for us to even attempt the flight. I pictured Jim choking when we tried to give him water, I imagined Luke coughing up blood, his rib having finally punctured his lung and I visualised sweet little Libby falling into a diabetic coma when her insulin ran out.

Finally, I fretted about my parents - they'd be worrying. I sat up fast, my parents! Wow, trumpets and fireworks moment!! Mum and Colin were, in my thoughts, bonded to one another, a pair – not my mother and her husband but my family. I got quite weepy as, for the first time, I thought of Colin as kin, not as an intruder who'd slunk into my life. He was a good guy, he'd be worried about me in a way my dad would not. I felt guilt and deep regret for all the times I'd spurned Colin's love, I needed the chance to tell him I loved him back. I hated the thought of him and Mum worrying, crying, grieving even, I had to succeed, I had to get us out of here as soon as possible.

I woke from my eventual, short, unsettled sleep demoralised. A black, despairing mood had settled on my shoulders, my eventual night-time determination and resolve had dissolved and trickled away. It was partially light and I knew I should get up, check the weather, check Jim but, cocooned in my blanket of apathy, the temptation to curl up tighter and stay where I was overwhelming. Eventually the pain in my shoulder, arm, hip and knee, from lying on the floorboards got me moving, I creaked and crunched upwards and stumbled stiffly to the window. It was fogged, I rubbed, fat snowflakes tumbled down but lazily, gently.

As I walked back towards the fire, Libby was scrambling over Sasha with exaggerated carefulness, wedging Malty under her arm to stop him scrabbling and waking her sister. Together we tiptoed to the door and tipped Malty outside. "I'm pleased you're going to save us Nate," Libby said, slipping her little hand into mine as we watched the dog snuffling through the snow. I smiled ruefully, I'd led everyone to pin their hopes on me, backing down now was not an option.

The others woke one by one soon afterwards but, though I willed it, Jim remained sleeping and unresponsive. "Breakfast first," said Emmi, seeing me staring at him, "give him just a bit longer."

We examined and discussed our rations and decided on plain Digestives crumbled into custard, which we'd make by mixing the powder with melted, warmed ice. It tasted as good as it sounds!

"I don't smell so great," lamented Harvey as he

ate his jam reddened custard.

"None of us do Harv," smiled Emmi. "We need to get out of here so we can all have a nice hot shower."

"And a hot chocolate and steak, eggs and cucumber," added Sasha.

After our poor excuse for a breakfast, we sent Harvey and the girls to play outside whilst Luke held his father's hand and Emmi filled the syringe with lukewarm water. The mood was grim. Watching Emmi fill the syringe was like observing a hangman preparing a noose. "Are you sure about this," Luke challenged, his eyes wide with fear.

"Your dad's not coming round Luke, his body will begin to shut down without water, that could happen today. We have to try this, we'll be as careful as we can." As Emmi knelt by Jim, Luke lurched up from the sofa and barged past me, stumbling out of the door.

Emmi held out the syringe to me – I'd hoped she was going to do it but didn't blame her for delegating the responsibility. I took it unenthusiastically; I knew there wasn't really a choice but there's a difference between watching someone die and being instrumental in their death. Everything in me was screaming not to do this to this poor helpless man, my hands were shaking.

Emmie and I looked at each other and she gave a tiny nod of her head. She put her fingers on Jim's lips and gently pulled his mouth open. I put the syringe to his lips. I closed my eyes and took a deep breath. Moved my thumb to the top of the plunger and opened my eyes. As I looked at Jim's face a film reel of images flitted before my eyes – his eyes gleaming with excitement as he takes delivery of the first parts for his plane, his patience as he explains the cockpit dials to me, the love in his eyes every time he looks at Luke, him goofing around dad dancing at Luke's birthday party.

Suddenly I jumped, snatching my hand away from his mouth, my eyes wide. Emmie started too and I thought she'd seen what I'd seen but her quizzical look told me she'd only been startled by my fright.

"I think his eyes just flickered," I breathed. Emmie looked sceptical but sympathetic. I knew what she was thinking – I was seeing what I wanted to see.

We both glued our eyes on Jim's, holding our breath and waiting what seemed an age but in reality, was probably only a few minutes. I was just about to admit I'd been wrong when it happened again, more definitively this time, both eye lids flickered then went still.

Emmie gave a broad grin then dashed out of the cabin, a few seconds later, she reappeared, trailing a charging Luke.

He looked at me, hope etched on his face then the three of us stared at his father. Like before, it took a little while but eventually Jim's eyelids flicked. "Oh, thank God," Luke breathed. "Dad, Dad, can you hear me." There was no indication that Jim could, but his eyelids continued to flicker on and off for the next ten minutes before his face became still again.

"What now?" Luke said.

"Well," I considered. Jim's best chance of survival was still us getting out of here and whilst we lingered in the cabin the plane was not fixing itself, but Luke could not be left to deal with this alone. "I think we should stay here and watch him for now. If he comes round, even for a brief moment, we can get some fluid safely into him."

The twins and Harvey drifted back inside and for the next hour we all stared at Jim. Time dragged, frustrated I got up to pace, the list of jobs to be done nagging insistently. Irritated, I walked outside and slapped the cabin wall, there were so many things to be achieved today and whilst we waited here they remained exasperatingly untouched. The weather was fine, I really needed to get out and work on that plane whilst I had a chance.

As I fretted and sulked Emmi yelled, I burst back through the door and dashed to the sofa. Jim's eyelids were flickering again and this time his fingers twitched too. As we watched, the movements became a little more pronounced until finally he opened his eyes.

"Dad, Dad, it's me, Luke." Jim burbled something but we couldn't make out any words and he didn't move.

"Let's get some water into him quickly whilst he's conscious," said Emmie.

"Yes," agreed Harvey, walking away from the

action. "People emerging from a coma can come and go for days before they regain consciousness properly. Take the chance and hydrate him when you can."

Emmi opened Jim's unresisting mouth and I trickled in a couple of drops of water. As she shut his mouth everyone held their breath but there were no signs of him choking. We repeated the process again several times until he'd had what we considered to be sufficient water – not much – but hopefully enough to keep him alive for now.

Luke bravely offered to keep giving water to Jim when he woke. He practised, left handed on me. His effort was far from deft, I ended up with a very soggy collar, but he would manage.

The rest of us booted and suited, collected the ready filled boat and set off for the plane.

Chapter 15

A watery sun hung low in the sky. It had no warmth, but it was lovely to see, inordinately welcome after the previous veil of grey cloud. The glorious orangey glow provided a perfect backdrop for the streamers of ice crystals clinging to branches and snowy overhangs. It lit the thick carpet of sugary, glittering virgin snow which undulated all around. The land we'd come down in was bleak and inhospitable, this morning it seemed almost magical. Our spirits were high. As we walked to the plane Harvey hummed loudly, tunelessly and we played a game of decoding animal tracks in the new snow: large half-moon ones, we decided were moose or caribou; small half-moon ones deer. Others could be hares or foxes, "or Woofles or Lumlegsters," suggested Sasha.

"Buffagoggles or Flufflets," asserted Libby.

My black mood had levered itself from me. In the daylight, my plan made sense again and I was invigorated, filled with unquenchable optimism and energy. The twins and Malty bounced around us, whooping and hollering, arms wind milling. When we reached the bank to the lake Sasha leapt off the top again, landing on her butt, feet out in front, careering down. She shot back up a small heap of snow at the foot of the bank, flew into the air and plunged back down on the lake – whoomph - a perfect face-plant, arms and legs sprawled, butt pointing to that blessedly bright sky.

"Might rescuers come for us today?" asked Libby. It was possible, as we walked I kept scanning the sky, I noticed the others were doing the same. Our eyes eventually began to sting and tear up from the brightness as we all gazed intently upwards as if we might be able to will an aircraft to appear at any moment.

"Think I've fried my eyeballs," moaned Sasha wiping her eyes with her sleeve. I lifted the bottom of my hat, uncovering my ears so I could more easily detect the distant drone of an approaching aeroplane engine or whop of helicopter blades.

"It would be great if they did reach us today," replied Emmi pragmatic as always, "but we should carry on with fixing the plane in case they don't."

We decided to search for the oil whilst the weather was good, the twins declared they would help before 'going to catch some fish for supper.' We spread out again and must have walked for about a kilometre. We kept changing places, swapping between inside and outside the forest, taking turns wading through the thick snow on the edge. "There are no more fallen branches," observed Emmi at last, I think we've passed the point where we must have started to hit the trees."

"And no oil," I remarked dejected – jeez, I felt like I was on an emotional roller-coaster - wildly upbeat one minute, despairing and defeated the next.

"Well," said Sasha, "if we can't leave here I definitely need to get back to fish catching. I'm sick of biscuits and snow melt custard is totally disgusting." She turned and began to wade back towards the plane. The rest of us trooped after her, shoulders slumped in misery.

"Got to go to the loo," declared Libby after a while, "can you wait for me please?"

"Sure," agreed Emmi. Then, as Libby trotted off

deeper into the forest. "Lib, just pick a spot, it's not like there's a shortage of trees to hide behind."

"I won't be able to go if I'm too close," called back Libby, then with a panicked "ohh," she disappeared out of sight.

"Libby?" Emmi yelled, running towards her, "what's happened? Where d'you go?"

"S'okay," Libby shouted, reappearing up in front of us, covered from head to foot in snow, "I was turning around to talk to you and I didn't see it, I just slipped in a bit, but I didn't fall down, there's a …, I don't know, a gulley thing."

We reached her and stood in a line, staring down the steep crevasse. "There's something down there," said Harvey pointing, "caught against that rock."

He was right. "Is it the oil?" asked Emmi. I shrugged; it was difficult to tell but there wasn't exactly a profusion of litter in these parts. In all likelihood the debris was an item from the spares box. If what we could see wasn't the oil, chances are it was down there too, not far off.

"We absolutely cannot climb down to look," declared Harvey, backing away from the edge, "it'd be very dangerous."

I shook my head, raising my palms in a 'can you believe it,' gesture. It was inconceivable that so many things could go wrong, we really were facing set back after set back.

"Could you tie me with the boat rope and lower me down?" asked Libby. I looked at Emmi, I couldn't make that decision. I could see from Emmi's face that she'd much rather have done it herself, I'd rather go over the top than Libby too but: one, Emmi and I were stronger than Libby to hold the rope at the top; and two, Libby would be lighter than us on the other end.

"We could give it a try," agreed Emmi with reluctance.

Rather than stand around in the cold waiting, we all trooped back to the boat to fetch the rope. Harvey was a big guy and it would have been useful to have him as an anchor-man at the end of the rope, but he declared he was going for a walk on the lake. Clearly, he couldn't deal with the possibility of injury any better than he could deal with actual injury, I didn't push it, I'd learned it wasn't worth it.

The rest of us headed back to the crevasse with the rope. We tied one end securely around Libby's waist and the other around mine and Emmi's. I made sure my gloves were on tight so that my grip would not slip, then we walked to the edge of the gulley in a line, Libby first, then me, with Emmi bringing up the rear. At the lip Libby turned her back to the crevasse and faced us, Sasha didn't follow but stood at a distance bouncing nervously from one foot to the other. "We've got you Lib," encouraged Emmi, "just go down nice and steady, see if the oil is down there and if it is, try to reach it. If you get scared or decide you can't do it don't worry, just yell and we'll pull you straight back up."

Libby nodded, gripped the rope, took a huge breath then lent back and pushed over the edge.

I was surprised at how difficult it was to support even her slight weight, I jammed my heals into the snow and strained, hearing Emmi grunt behind me as she did the same thing. I could still see Libby, fine powder trickled from the lip of the crevasse where the rope disturbed it onto her head, surrounding her in a dusty white cloud. She looked up at me, her eyes wide. "You can do it Libby." Her mouth lifted in a tiny, forced smile then she began to heel down the crevasse.

"Can you see the oil Libby?" I yelled when the rope was almost completely extended.

"I'm not sure," came back the shaky reply. "I've got my eyes shut," we all giggled, despite the tension.

"Might need to open them now Lib," suggested Emmi.

A few more inches of rope then, "there are some other things here, definitely things from the plane, but I can't see the oil. There's some more stuff a little lower down, you'll need to lower me further so I can check them out."

I played out the last bit of rope, "more," shouted Libby.

"We'll need to move forward," I said over my shoulder to Emmi and we shuffled a couple of steps closer to the edge of the crevasse, then a few more.

"Yess," shouted Libby, "I can see the oil, but I

188

can't quite reach it."

Emmi and I shuffled a few centimetres more, "no closer," I warned, "we don't know what's solid ground and what's just an overhang of snow. Can you reach the bottle now Libby?"

"No," she wailed. "My arm's not long enough to reach down and I can't quite hook it with my feet. If I untied my waist and dangled on the rope by my hands for a few seconds I'm sure I could get it between my feet."

"No!" the rest of us yelled together."

"Don't do that Libby," Sasha warned urgently dashing to the edge of the crevasse and lying on her belly to hang over so she could see her sister, "it's far too dangerous. Please Nate, Emmi, can you just pull her up, I don't like this at all"

Then before we could do so, "She's done it," Sasha squealed, "she's not tied on, she's just dangling."

"Oh God no." moaned Emmi, but she was sensible enough to maintain her position holding the rope. "Libby," she called urgently, "you must hold very tightly to that rope with both hands, we're pulling you up right now."

"She's got it," yelled Sasha, "don't pull yet, she's putting the oil inside her jacket. Okay, she's got both hands on the rope now."

Emmi and I pulled and pulled and pulled, as smoothly as we could. It was really, really difficult, my arms and shoulders were aching, even my back complained at the strain. Sasha came over and pulled with us and eventually Libby's head appeared over the top of the ridge, then she was lying on the top, waving the oil over her head like a trophy.

"Oh!" cried Sasha, hurling herself on top of her sister, "Libby, don't ever do anything like that again.

"Yeah, don't," panted Emmi and I in agreement, spread-eagled on the snow.

Chapter 16

Back at the plane I topped up the oil without incident. The girls were fishing again, Harvey was nowhere to be seen. "Right," said Emmi, "let's hope this wheel change is just as straightforward."

"Yeah," I agreed, "and as quick." The pleasant weather had been short-lived, the warm, pale yellow sunlight had faded, the light was, once again flat and white and dark, threatening clouds were swooping towards us as though someone were pulling a great dirty grey curtain across the sky.

It started out well, we cleared away the soft snow and piled three rounds of tree trunk on top of each other on the firm base. Too high, we removed a log and replaced it with a thinner one, swapping the different thicknesses until the pile looked about the right height for leverage. I placed the fence post horizontally over the logs and see-sawed it experimentally backwards and forwards, adjusting the fulcrum. Emmi shook her head, "not quite right," she said, so we wriggled the trunk sections backwards a few inches and tried again.

Emmi nodded and wedged the pointed end of the fence post under the tail of the plane, I pushed down on the top end of the fence post and the tail lifted, raising the broken wheel off the ground. Emmi manoeuvred the sawhorse under the tail and there it was, all jacked up and ready to work on.

Removing the wheel was not quite so simple, the spanners in the toolbox were too big for the nuts that held the wheel. I tried and tried but could not get any to grip. "Don't take your outer gloves off," warned Emmi. I wasn't going to, I'd been there and done that and could still feel the pain just thinking about it. It was really cold again, now the heavy clouds had begun to shed their load and the first few flakes were tumbling from the sky.

Clumsy in my thick gloves, I tried some more to get purchase on the nuts with the spanner. Emmi disappeared; I could hear her scrabbling around in the canoe. "Push these in, one either side," she suggested, returning to my side, handing me two flat blade screwdrivers.

"Hey," I smiled as the spanner caught

immediately over the top of the screwdrivers. "You really are the Queen of Improvisation." It was slow going, I had to take the spanner off and reposition it on top of the screwdrivers on every turn, but it was working, eventually the bent wheel and twisted bracket were removed.

The fitting of the snowboard was going well until I handed Emmi the last of the bolts to attach the bracket and she informed me we were one short. "I thought I'd placed them all carefully on the top of our tree trunk jack until we re-used them," she said miserably, "I knew if one fell in the snow we'd have trouble finding it again."

"Perhaps it just rolled off," I replied, kneeling and sifting through the soft snow around the tree trunks.

No bolt. "If I dropped it when I was carrying it over, one of us could have kicked it," Emmi groaned, "and all the snow's been mussed about by our boots, it could take ages to find."

"Better get started looking then," declared Harvey, as he re-joined us. The three of us crawled about on our hands and knees riffling through the snow with our fingers. It took ages, during which time the weather went from bad to worse. All of a sudden there was a yell from the lake.

"Oh Lord," cried Emmi, bolting upright and dashing towards the lake, "Sasha, Libby, what's happened."

I heard one of the girls shriek a reply but couldn't catch what she said, Harvey and I were rushing through the snow after Emmi. My heart was in my mouth, what new disaster had befallen us? – had one of the girls fallen through the ice?

Apparently not, Libby, then Sasha appeared at the top of the bank, "come quickly," Sasha yelped. We followed them onto the lake and there lay a large fish, twisting and thumping pathetically. Malty was beside it, bouncing in excitement towards it then leaping back in fright.

"I caught one," said Sasha, her voice a mixture of pride and horror, "but it didn't die, it's just thrashing about, it's horrible, please do something." Harvey had taken one look at the poor creature and turned tail, Emmi and I looked at each other.

I shook my head, repairing and flying a plane were things I was capable of, killing a creature was not. Emmi looked a little sick, "no?"

"Sorry, I absolutely can't," I replied.

"If we didn't really need some real food I'd pop the poor thing back in the lake," she agreed, "but I guess desperate times call for this desperate measure. Right," she sucked in a breath, nodded to herself then took reluctant, slow motion steps towards the fish. She stood, looking down at it, "Gotta be done," I heard her mutter, "ooh hoo hoo, gotta be done." Another deep breath and nod to herself and she took hold of the fish's tail, closed her eyes, swung it high and dashed it hard down on the ice. The crunch was sickening, Emmi dropped it immediately and scuttled backwards, stopping a few feet away.

"Eeugh, eeugh, eeugh," she squealed, hugging herself, "nasty, nasty, nasty." I watched her steel herself and walk hesitantly back to the fish, "please, please, please God let it be dead." It apparently was, "thank you, a million, trillion thank yous!" she gasped skywards. Averting her eyes, she picked it up gingerly by the tail and carried it at arms-length up the bank.

"Is it dead," enquired Sasha, peering out from behind Libby. Emmi nodded grimly, I think she was still a little too freaked out to risk speaking. The girls shuddered, "I thought they just died when you fished them out of the water," explained Sasha in horror, "I didn't realise it would lie there suffering then have to be killed."

"Well, it's done now," Emmi replied, in a slightly squeaky voice, "really well done catching it, we can have it for supper."

"Umm," said Libby, "could you put it somewhere, do you think? Where we can't see it." Emmi looked around, spotted a pile of drifted snow and popped the fish down behind it.

The snow was really bleaching down hard now, everyone was white coated. "Back to that bolt," suggested Emmi, keen to move her mind to something other than the fish. "Look, I guess we'll need to dig out the piled snow from under and in front of the plane so we can get it onto the lake before we can leave anyway, let's do it very carefully and look for the bolt as we go."

We took turns with the shovel, the rest of us scooping up armfuls of snow and moving it from the plane's path. Since it was snowing hard it felt a little like bowling a ball up-hill, but I knew any newly fallen snow would be much easier to move before we left than the hard, piled heap it had ploughed ahead of it when we crashed.

Keeping my eyes peeled for the missing bolt, I soon lost myself in the monotony of the task – shovel or scoop, move and dump. Even though it was hard physical work I was getting cold and darkness was fast approaching, I knew we needed to get back to the cabin soon. I was very close to believing the bolt was gone for good when Harvey found it. He tucked it in his pocket whilst we finished clearing the path to the top of the bank. Once we'd done, I fumbled the bolt on with cold fingers, then we removed the sawhorse and re-loaded the canoe, adding the fish.

Through the fast falling flakes, hunched, teeth chattering we regarded the plane solemnly. "So," Emmi said, "it's ready."

"Yep," I agreed, "good to go."

"So, when do we leave?"

"Soon, I guess." Emmi shook her head, put her hands on her hips and looked me straight in the eye in that disconcerting way of hers. Okay, vagaries weren't going to get me by, it was commitment time.

"First thing tomorrow morning," I said. "We fly first thing tomorrow, weather permitting."

Chapter 17

Jim had had several periods of semi-wakefulness, Luke reported. He'd managed to get some water into him each time. Whilst clearly still very much in pain, Luke was much more cheerful, more hopeful for his father and happy to have a job to do. He oohed and aahed over the fish and congratulated us on having got the plane ready.

We cooked the fish in a dish over the fire, the twins staring at it, poking it every now and then, lifting a little flap of skin to see if it was done. "Is it ready Emmi? Now? Now?" When it was, the twins carried it proudly between them, using socks, hopefully clean but probably not, as oven gloves. They placed it with reverence on the table in front of us.

Harvey refused to eat any, "no way I'm eating anything that's been alive, even if I am very, very hungry," but Luke shuffled across to the table so the rest of us could eat together. Luke and Sasha squashed on one of the two chairs, Emmi and Libby on the other, I balanced precariously on two of our make-shift jack tree trunks.

"We are sorry fish, for ending your life," said Sasha bowing her head, "but you died in a good cause."

"You are a hero fish," added Libby. "You gave your life to save ours."

Fish was far from my favourite food, in fact I'm not sure I'd ever eaten one without having asked 'do I really have to Mum?' This fish, however, was flaky, pearly white, and succulent. After three days of eating what Mum would call 'rubbish,' this tasted like the most delicious food I'd ever put in my mouth.

"Mmhmf," groaned Emmi, closing her eyes and chewing slowly, savouring every mouthful. I concurred, definitely 'mmhmf.' Aside from that there was complete silence, everyone focused on their meal. I swung my gaze over them, my old and new friends and grinned. We were a ragged little bunch, we all had a rather wild, abandoned look by now, even the super tidy Emmi. Our hair, which none of us had bothered to brush, was mussed and tatted by our bobble hats and above the smell of fish a sweaty, boiled onion aroma prevailed.

We had more snow melt custard with crumbled biscuits and the last of the Kendal Mint Cake for afters, then retired to the fire. There was an unusual, strained kind of silence now. I knew each of us was contemplating how seriously everything hung in the balance. If the weather was reasonable we would leave here in the morning. There was a brutal realisation that this time tomorrow we could just as easily be dead as alive. That the fish, lovely as it was, could be our last ever meal was a terrifying thought.

Gradually, I became aware that everyone was staring at me. I'd heard Luke speak but was so absorbed by my own thoughts I'd not registered what he was saying. I cast around in my mind and hooked his question from the depths of my brain. It was a simple but fundamental one – "Are you sure you can do it?"

Everyone waited. As before, I knew what they needed me to say, so I swallowed my doubts once again and conjured up a smile. "I can," I nodded, "As soon as there's a slot in the weather, I can fly us out of here. Look, it's a gamble, I'll give you that, but it's a carefully calculated one. I sincerely believe I can do it;

I wouldn't risk my life or anyone else's if I didn't."

"I'm going to be your First Officer?" declared Emmi, "I'll be right there beside you in the cockpit. I can work the radio and do anything else you tell me to do. Unless you'd rather I didn't, I can just sit in the cabin with the others," she finished as I stared at her.

"No. No," I reassured her quickly. "It would really help to have your support up front. Thanks Emmi."

"Can you talk me through some stuff?"

"Sure." I replied. "We can go through the manuals now, then I can take you through the dials in the cockpit tomorrow before we leave."

"I'd rather we just stayed here," said Harvey, looking forlorn.

"I know Harv," Emmi patted his hand in sympathy, "but won't it be great to see Mum and Dad, they'll have been so worried about us."

"Suppose," agreed Harvey half-heartedly, far from convinced.

"I can't wait to show them our souvenirs," Sasha, beamed round us, desperate for us to ask.

202

"What souvenirs?" I obliged. Libby unwrapped a scarf and displayed their treasures with pride – the twisted stirrup from the tail wheel, the empty oil canister, a handful of fish bones, a crumpled drawing of us all round the fire – Jim looked dead in it - and several small frozen brown balls.

"Mum and Dad will love them," agreed Emmi, "but you do know that that deer poo won't be frozen by the time we reach them don't you?!"

Chapter 18

That night, I lay sleepless on the hard floor once again. I could hear a lot of shuffling around me, whispering between the girls, I don't think anyone was sleeping. I checked my watch; five past two, twenty-five to three, ten past three, marvellous, it was going to be a long one!

At 4.30am the hail began to spit against the windows, fifteen minutes later and it was beating loudly against the roof, the wind rattling the windows, 'get it over with,' I thought falling into a restless doze.

An hour later conditions had not improved. We were all up and the girls and I were pacing the floor, strung out and irritable, taking turns to open the door to check roughly every twenty-five seconds! No one had been able to face breakfast. I felt maddened by frustration, the weather – our constant enemy, "give us a break will you?" I yelled upwards out of the door. We really needed to go, the longer we hung around the more the doubt settled in, fear whispered at the edges of my mind, much longer and I'd bottle out of the whole thing. Jim was 'waking' more frequently now, and I couldn't help wondering if we waited another day would he come round properly? At least be able to talk me through the flight if he couldn't manage it himself.

After much deliberating, I decided I wouldn't risk missing a break in the weather to wait and see. After tomorrow morning Libby would be out of insulin, we just didn't have the luxury of hanging around. Jim might regain consciousness within the next twenty-four hours, but he might not. Either way, if we missed a weather slot today there just might not be another tomorrow.

"I think it's easing," said Emmi at last. The twins and I charged over to join her at the open door. She was right, the falling flakes were fewer and smaller and there was a little more light in the day. The visibility was still too poor to take off in though.

"Good," I replied, "are we all ready to leave if it clears sufficiently?"

"All packed up and good to go," chirped Emmi brightly, like we were leaving a guest house at the end of a weekend's break in Blackpool. "Everything's there ready to throw in the canoe," she pointed to a heap by the door. "We just need to get that, then Mr Carter in at the last moment."

"You and I could head over to the plane now," I suggested. "I could talk you through the instrument panel, show you how to use the radios and go through the take-off and landing procedures."

"Good plan Batman," said Sasha. "Luke, Libby and I can watch some more Barbie whilst we wait."

I had noticed that the twins loved being with Luke and that even Harvey, who didn't really like people, was drawn to him. I felt no surprise at this, it was what always happened at home – people flocked round him like moths to a flame. What confused me was that Emmi seemed indifferent to his charms. I asked her about it as we walked to the plane. She gave my question much thought – you always knew you were going to get a considered answer from Emmi, never a trite brush-off. "Luke's great," she explained at last, "but he's too …. much. Sure, he's lively and funny and super cute," I felt my heart sink a little at that, "but he's like some boy god presiding over the rest of us, he's inconsistent, a bit of a tempest, he makes me a little nervous. You," she continued, "are much more authentic, more normally flawed. You're more steadfast and dependable, I'm much more comfortable with you."

"Thanks," I said, "I think!" Steadfast and dependable! – made me sound like Colin. Still, she preferred me to Luke, that was unheard of. Unheard of, totally unexpected and good to know. Very, very good to know.

When we reached the plane, I led Emmi to the wings. "These," I said, touching a hinged section at the back of the wings, "are flaps. Pilots use these to adjust the wing's curvature. You can take-off and land at much slower speeds with them out, also fly slower before stalling and falling from the sky. On take-off they provide greater lift and when you're landing, the increased drag helps slow a plane down. A good pilot doesn't need flaps out to land, they control their speed so that they approach sufficiently slowly to touch down. Poor pilots use them to slow the plane when they are coming in faster than they should be. I, of course, will need them big style! I gave a rueful grin. "So, I'll extend them for take-off, help us get off the ground. After takeoff, as the aircraft increases its speed, I'll retract the flaps and use these," I indicated the wing's other moving parts – "the ailerons - to make the aircraft turn or bank. Pushing an aileron increases the curvature of that wing, giving it more lift than the other and causing the plane to turn in the direction of the lower wing."

We climbed on board and entered the cockpit, Emmi recoiled as she took in the mind-boggling array of dials and switches. "I know," I grinned, "it's a bit daunting but you don't need to learn the function of everything. Look," I pointed to a group of dials, clustered in a T shape, in the centre of the dashboard, "these are the most important instruments." A white box had been painted around them, "pilots often group and highlight them like that so that their attention is drawn automatically to them.

This one here, I tapped a dial, is the Air Speed Indicator – we need to keep the needle in the green zone as we fly.

"Green zone, right," Emmi nodded.

"This one's the Attitude Indicator – the artificial horizon - it calculates a plane's position in relation to the horizon, see, the bottom half is brown for the earth, the top half blue for the sky, there are little wings in the middle," I pointed, "we need to keep those wings level so we know we're flying flat."

"Wings level on the Attitude Indicator."

"The next dial is the Altimeter."

"Tells us our altitude?" guessed Emmi

"Right and this one's just a compass, I'm sure you know what that does. Alongside the instruments in the white T are the Vertical Speed Indicator – which will tell us our rate of climb or descent, the fuel gauge, oil pressure and oil temperature gauge, and engine RPM indicator," I tapped each dial in turn. "We'll need to keep an eye on that oil temperature because we've got far less oil than we should have in the engine. The ideal temperature is between sixty and seventy-five degrees Celsius. Ours will get hotter than that, we just need to make sure the needle doesn't climb too high. At ninety-five degrees there'll be engine damage."

"Watch the oil temperature gauge," Emmie muttered, mentally storing the information.

"When we get on board it would be great if you could run me through the checklists and once we are up you can try to reach someone on the radio. During the flight it would be great to have a second pair of eyes monitoring the dials."

An hour and a half later Emmi and I burst back through the door of the cabin. Outside there was patchy blue sky and a windless silence. "Okay troops, this is it, we're good to go," Emmi beamed, though I could tell from the tension in her body and the worry clouding her eyes that her jolliness was very much put on.

The others pulled on their coats, salopettes, boots, hats and gloves slowly and sombrely, like they were completing a ritual, then Emmi, Harvey and I hauled Jim's deadweight off the sofa as carefully we could. As we lifted him his eyes opened, and he gave a loud grunt and struggled against us. We hadn't expected it and dropped him, by good fortune back onto the sofa, in surprise.

"Jim," I called.

"Dad," Luke yelled, but Jim was still, we'd lost him again.

We lifted him once more and manhandled him out of the door and into the canoe. I took one last look around the cabin before shutting the door, the note the girls had left on the table for the owners fluttered in the breeze. 'We are sorry to have broken the window of your cabin,' they had written, 'and apologise for sawing the porch railings and pulling down your guttering but we were desperate because our plane crashed. We had to take your boat to transport Mr Carter because he is in a coma and it is too far to carry him, we will leave it on the lake bank for you - just turn to the right and walk across the lake. No, it will probably not be properly frozen by the time you get here, don't walk on it, it will be unsafe, walk around it until you come to the boat. We are also sorry for taking down your curtains, but my sister and I needed a blanket and our brother needed a den.' They'd made us each sign our name and had snapped a pen and added an inky thumb print from Jim and paw print from Malty.

"Where's Harvey?" Emmi asked as I joined

them by the canoe.

"On grumpy street," replied Sasha, lobbing a snowball at me. I didn't bother to duck; she was a rubbish shot. "Anyone want one last icicle before we leave?"

"He's around the back of the cabin," elucidated Libby, "I don't think he wants to go; he seems quite sad."

"Give me a minute," Emmi waded through the fresh snow towards the rear of the cabin. When she hadn't returned five minutes later I followed her round.

"But I don't get my headaches here," Harvey was saying heartbreakingly. "I don't get panicked or confused, it's so slow and quiet and … constant. Life is too fast for me, too complex and demanding. It rushes past so quickly I can't get hold of it, I'm still trying to make sense of one thing when three more things have happened, it's scary."

"Oh Harvey," Emmi's voice caught. "I hate it that everything is so hard for you, but I can't leave without you. I love you so much and so do Mum and Dad, they will be desperate to see you. I need you to come with us. Besides you haven't got any red food left here."

Harvey sighed and nodded, shoulders hunched in misery. Together we collected the canoe, waded back through the soft, freshly fallen snow to the bank and began our final trek across the lake. No one spoke, there was little left to say. Luke laboured alongside me, his breathing was loud and ragged but he seemed to be finding walking less painful than he had when we'd headed to the cabin three days ago.

For safety, we left Jim in the canoe on the edge of the lake, covered by a pile of clothing to keep him warm, whilst we moved the plane. I had brought the paddle and the sweeping brush, I used them to gently loosen, then sweep the snow from the wings. Once it was off I removed my gloves and swept the heel of my hand quickly over the metal. Damn! I'd hoped they'd be clear but there was a very thin layer of stubbornly stuck, solid ice under the snow that we'd have to remove.

"It's all got to come off," I explained, "the wings need to be entirely ice free. We can't risk taking off with any on there at all. Ice on the wings will increase drag and reduce lift, resulting in a longer take-off roll and a slower climb rate. This lake is only just long enough for a runway as it is, I need to get the plane in the air as quickly as I can."

"Can we hack it off with the paddle, or, I don't know, go back and get some hot water to pour over it or something?" asked Emmi.

I shook my head, "the wings are just aluminium, they're fairly fragile, we can't risk scraping and banging them hard in case we damage them and the water would make the problem worse. The metal is so cold, the water, no matter how hot, would freeze very quickly when it touched them."

"How are you going to clear them then?" asked Luke, sitting on the snow, cradling his arm.

Hmmm, good question, I looked around for inspiration and spotted the remains of the beacon we'd built but never lit. I spun slowly in a circle, gauging the wind. 'Yep, that would work.' "It'll take a while, but we could move that pile of wood to the front left of the plane and light a fire, the wind's in the right direction to blow the hot air over the wings."

"Let's get started then," agreed Emmi. As we built the fire I scanned the sky for signs of the bad weather returning 'Please, please, please let it hold,' I prayed, I couldn't imagine missing the slot and having to return to the cabin now.

The sky remained a clear grey/blue. When the bonfire was constructed I grabbed an armful of clothing and thrust it into Emmi's arms, beckoning to her to follow me.

The plane had three fuel tanks along the bottom of the fuselage, on the underside of each was a drain valve, designed to allow a pilot to check the fuel was free from water. "Hold the clothes under here." Emmi did as I asked, I opened the valve and she let the fuel soak the clothes. We took them back to the fire and pushed them in between the branches, then Harvey touched them with a match. They burned quickly and the wood caught with relative ease. To help the hot air along we took off our coats and wafted them towards the wings. Twenty minutes later we were red faced, coughing and stinking of smoke but the wings of the

215

plane were perfectly ice free.

Re-clearing the path to the lake bank was a fairly quick job. We'd discussed the best way to get the plane onto the lake - pushing it the short distance to the top of the bank wouldn't be a problem, it would slide along quite easily on its skis, but the slope down to the lake was steep, I didn't want the plane careering down nose first and getting damaged. Harvey came up with the solution: there were trees to either side of the plane on the lake bank, a single tree a few meters away on the left side and a small cluster a little further along on the right. We could tie two pieces of rope, one on each side, to the strong front wheel fairings, loop it around the trees and let the plane, hand over hand gently down onto the lake.

My main worry was the propeller, if it hit the ice it would all be over, even the smallest bit of damage would stop us flying out of here. I turned it so one blade was vertical, pointing to 12 o'clock and the other two were horizontal, that was the best I could do to protect it.

I led Libby to the back of the plane and looped a

rope around the tail. "Your job is to keep the tail down," I said

Libby pinned her arms to her sides, refusing to take the rope, "I'll never be able to hold it," she panicked.

I smiled at her, "don't worry, your job won't be to slow the plane, just to stop it tipping. All the weight's behind the front wheels, the plane is designed to stay upright, even your little bit extra pull should keep that tail down."

Things did not quite go to plan! We pushed the plane to the top of the bank with ease, then Sasha and Luke, who insisted he helped despite our protests, rocked the plane until it tipped over the lip. Once over, it went down hard. Even with the friction and leverage of the tree trunks and our combined weight, Harvey on one rope and Emmi and I on the other, we were no match for the plane's trajectory. We slowed its descent by a fraction, but it was still way too fast. Poor Libby gave a yell and flew forwards, nose diving into the snow before dropping the rope, the plane pitched forwards before coming upright again. I hurtled down the bank, pausing to make sure a snow-covered Libby was okay. I hesitated at the water's edge, scared to step on the lake in case the ice suddenly broke, the plane had hit it hard and I worried it may have cracked. I looked and listened, straining my eyes and ears but I could neither see nor hear any creaking or cracking. Still I waited a few minutes, expecting the plane to be swallowed up by a swell of water any moment.

Finally, I stepped tentatively onto the ice and walked to front of the plane, fearing the worst. Luck was on our side though- the propeller was still in the same position and was undamaged. "All good," I yelled, giving a relieved thumbs-up to the group anxiously looking on from the bank.

Everyone trailed me around the outside of the plane as I performed a final external inspection, looking for any damage that may have been hidden by the snow banked under the plane. "Still all good." We stood in a silent, sober line, staring at the plane, all reluctant to take the giant leap of climbing on board. 'Would this metal cylinder be the instrument of our salvation or our death?'

'In the future,' I thought, 'if there is a future for me, I'll be sitting grey haired and wrinkly in a care home and this is the memory that will jump into my mind. This is the definitive image of our time here, the one that will remain imprinted on my brain – six scared, ragged children standing on the ice by a battered airplane, all infinitesimally small in the surrounding, vast snowy wilderness.'

I pulled off my scarf and held it in the air above my head, it gave a half-hearted flutter, then flopped down my back. "very little wind," I muttered.

"That's a good thing, right?" asked Emmi.

"Uh, uh," Harvey shook his head, "strong headwind would be better, we'd be able to take off with a slower ground speed, would be less in danger of running out of lake before we were going fast enough to get into the air."

"Makes no sense," Emmi frowned.

Luke snuffled a laugh, "Just remembering your first ever visit to my house, your 'principles of flight lesson.' I found it all so dull, could never understand why you wanted to know. I'm pleased you kept your interest now though."

I grinned at him, remembering too. My eyes filled and my throat clogged, Jim had been so patient with me, had given me so much of his time over the years. I squared my shoulders, he'd taught me well, now was the time to put it all into practice, pay him back by getting him safely out of here. I turned to Emmi to explain, "the air bearing down on the plane as it accelerates forwards generates an upwards force on the wings which lifts the aircraft. If you have a strong headwind, say thirty knots, your groundspeed can be thirty knots less before that lift is generated - the wind gives you a boost."

Emmi nodded, "but we've not got a headwind, so no help?"

"No, but at least we've not got a tailwind. It could be worse."

"So, will we get up before we reach the end of the lake?" asked Luke.

"Should do. Luckily for us, the Otter, is a STOL, a short take-off and landing plane. Take-off distance is just five hundred meters for this plane, that's five hundred meters to be fifty meters above ground, by my reckoning, the lake's slightly longer than that." What I held back was that five hundred meters was the distance a land plane needed to get off the ground, a ski plane required five hundred and sixty meters. Our plane was now a hybrid, I wasn't entirely sure what implication that had on our required take-off distance but since the lake, by my rough calculation was less than six hundred meters long it was going to be tight. All we could do was give it a try; I'd abort if I wasn't up to speed in time.

We towed Jim in the canoe to the plane, pushed, shoved and hauled him on-board and strapped him in a seat.

The cabin was still littered with the carnage of the spilled contents of bags and suitcases. Everyone stared wide eyed and silent, reliving the crash – it was a reminder we could do without at this particular moment! Hastily I got down on my hands and knees and began raking everything together, stuffing it randomly and haphazardly back inside the luggage. The spell that had rooted everyone to the spot, winding memories of fear and horror through their heads, broke and the others pitched in to help. We cleared the cabin and stored the cases back behind the torn cargo net, securing it as best we could with the rope and some scarfs.

Harvey shut the plane door and he, Luke and the twins settled themselves in their seats, Sasha holding tightly onto Malty. Everyone was silent. Fear and uncertainty had returned to haunt me with a vengeance. I felt sick and sweaty, my stomach churned, and my legs were shaky as Emmi and I headed for the cockpit.

As I buckled myself in the left-hand seat doubt slunk around me, a great black shadow slipping over my shoulder, spreading like oil on water until I was submerged in it. I couldn't focus, the dials and switches - a dizzying, terrifying array - pulsed and swarmed before my eyes. Though I knew the purpose of each, my mind was blank, I hadn't a clue what to do first. I picked up the manual and flicked, in panic, through the long checklists, nothing was making any sense at all.

"Are we nearly there yet?" Luke's voice reached me from the cabin, the others laughed -a high, nervous sound but laughter, nevertheless. Good old Luke, doing what he did best, making everything better. I smiled and closed my eyes. As I relaxed, everything Jim had taught me flooded back, I sorted it quickly. Though I was still shaking and sweating in the intense cold I was ready now.

I reached over and handed the manual to Emmi, "can you read the checklists now?"

"Sure," she began to read from the long list:

"Parking Brake."

"Set," I replied, my voice a little squeaky.

"Throttle." I examined the levers on the dashboard, there were three – 'which one, which one?'

"Take your time," Emmi said gently, "you can do this."

I took a deep breath, looked again and identified the throttle, "idle," I confirmed.

"Set Propeller to high RPM."

I located the variable pitch propeller lever, another of the three, and switched it to high. "Propeller set to high RPM," I responded.

"Fuel Flow/Mixture."

This would regulate the percentage of oxygen to fuel flowing through the engine, too rich (too much fuel) and the engine would be too cold, too lean (too much oxygen) and the engine would get hot. I checked the switch, "set to cut-off."

Emmi nodded and continued, listing the switches for me to check, man...there were a lot of them:

"Battery and Alternator Switches."

"Off."

"Magneto Switch."

"Off."

"Starter Switch."

"Off."

"Fuel Boost Pump Switch."

"Off."

"Pitot Heat."

"Off."

"Carburettor Heat."

"Off."

"Battery Switch."

"On."

"Panel light."

"On."

"Flaps."

"Up."

"Phew, do pilots go through this every time they take off," asked Emmi, blowing out her cheeks.

"They do, no matter how many times they've done it before. Should be nearly at the end now," I reassured her.

"Flight Controls," she continued.

I pushed the control column forwards, pulled it back, tilted it left, then right, "free and full movement of the control column," I confirmed. "Checking rudders," I pressed both pedals, neither jammed, "rudders okay."

"Elevator Trim," Emmi said. I looked at her blankly, "set for take-off it says," she shrugged.

I scanned the dials and switches, none said 'elevator trim,' I felt myself beginning to panic again. I took a deep breath, closed my eyes and transported myself back to White Horse, visualising Jim in my seat. "Aha," I had it. I reached above my head and turned a wheel until it said, 'Set for take-off.' "Done," I said with a sigh of relief.

"Fuel quantities," Emmi said.

I shrugged, "we've got what we've got." We'd re-fuelled before we came down and Jim had put extra fuel on-board in case we had to divert. "We'll be fine to make it to Old Crow"

"Emmi nodded. "Fuel tank selector."

There were three tanks in the centre of the plane under the floor, "switched to fullest tank," I said.

"Clock."

"Set."

"Radios."

"On."

"GPS."

GPS!! I'd searched for a working iPad to check our location when we'd come down, there'd been GPS right here in the cockpit all along! Oh well, knowing where we were would have changed nothing. I switched on the system and input our destination, watched as the navigation system mapped our route. "On," I replied, "route calculated."

"Transponder."

"Standby."

"Beacon."

"On."

"Pre-flight checks complete and satisfactory," Emmi gave a thumbs up, I could see her hands were shaking a little.

I tried and failed to give her a smile of reassurance. "Pre-start up checklist now," Emmi flicked some pages and began. As before, we ran through each of the checks, then I opened the throttle a fraction and switched on the fuel pump. With an unsteady hand, I reached out and pressed the starter motor. I stared at the oil pressure dial and held my breath, letting it out as the needle rose as it should.

A short while later and we'd trawled through the before taxi checklist too.

Getting used to the rudder pedals, I turned us in a jerky, uneven arc, 'lightly on the controls, both hands and feet,' I heard Jim's voice in my head. Slowly, at only about five miles per hour, I taxied to the widest part of the lake to give myself the maximum length of 'runway.' I used the brake to stop the plane so that we could run through the 'before take-off checklist.'

As Emmi read the list, I set the mixture - the percentage of oxygen to fuel- to rich, set the elevator trim and flaps for take-off and checked the flight controls and engine instruments again. I set the transponder to 1200, the code for visual flight and we were done.

As we finished, the dials began swimming in front of my eyes and once more I was drowning in a quicksand of fear. I felt out of breath, a hot flush dashed through my body and I started to sweat even more copiously, until my hands were slippery on the control column. I had a dim awareness of Emmi speaking to me, but it sounded as though her voice was coming from a long way away and I couldn't focus or pick out any of the words. I realised a large part of me had been hoping for a problem, hoping we'd find something that would mean we needed to abort our flight, but all the checks were complete, everything was in order, we were good to go.

'Calm down, calm down,' I lectured myself. I gulped in air until I managed to get myself back under some control. Emmi watched me but didn't comment, just gave me time to pull myself together. I mentally reviewed what Jim had told me about taking off in a tail-dragger – 'you need to very quickly push the nose down with the control column,' he'd said, 'get that tail up fast, it should be lifting at about thirty knots.'

I wiped my disgusting, sweating palms on my salopettes and nodded at Emmi, this was it. "Ready for take-off."

"Ladies and gentlemen," shouted Emmi down the cabin, with an admirable attempt at humour, "we are about to depart, please make sure your personal belongings are carefully stowed, your seats are upright, and your seat belts fastened."

I opened the throttle as smoothly as my shaking hands would allow, the engine roared and we accelerated, rocketing across the smooth surface of the lake. I watched the speed climb, just before we reached thirty knots I pushed the control column forwards and at exactly the same time the snowboard hit something, probably a lump of ice, on the otherwise smooth surface of the lake. There was a loud tearing sound and the plane's nose pitched violently forwards, the propeller skimming just above the ice. I panicked and pulled back hard on the control column, which tipped the plane in the opposite direction. The tail hit the ground, the now bare legs of the landing gear scraping harshly on the ice. For a second, I thought it was all over before it had begun, that we'd failed even before take-off. I'd never get up enough speed to take off before I reached the end of the lake with drag from the trailing legs slowing me down. By some stroke of luck however the tail bounced back up and stayed there, off the ground. Shaking with such violence my teeth chattered, I continued to throttle forwards, gripping the control column so tightly my hands hurt, before remembering Jim's words and forcing myself to ease my hold. Beside me Emmi gripped her seat arms, her eyes were tight shut and her lips moved in silent prayer.

The opposite bank loomed terrifyingly close, the plane ate up the distance. We'd reach our take off speed of eighty knots within about ten to fifteen seconds, but time was running in ultra-slow motion, forty knots, sixty. Closer and closer we rushed, too close, we weren't going to make it. I was about to pull back on the throttle when Emmi yelled "Rotate." We'd hit take off speed, we were going up. I went to haul back on the control column and stopped myself just in time – 'lightly, lightly,' I muttered. I gently pulled back and we lifted, clearing the lake bank by no more than a few feet. My heart leaped in my chest and I gasped for air, unaware I'd been holding my breath.

I grinned, forgetting the danger for a brief moment and giving myself up to the magic of the moment – I was flying. I was actually flying a plane. Elation flooded my body, I laughed out loud. I could hear cheering from the cabin, clapping hands, stamping feet. "You did it, you did it," yelled Emmi.

We climbed rapidly. Above the patchy clouds the sky was a crystal-clear blue – we could do this, we were headed back to civilisation. As soon as we were high enough out of the valley for the mountains not to be blocking the radio signal I asked Emmi to begin broadcasting on the emergency GUARD frequency. "Mayday, mayday, mayday," she called into the radio, "this is Charlie-Alpha-Delta-X-ray-Hotel requesting urgent assistance."

Nothing. "Did you release the button on the radio? Remember you need to do that to hear a response."

"Oops, no, forgot." Still no reply. "I thought there'd be planes out looking for us whilst the weather's clear, why can't we reach anyone?" asked Emmi, worry evident in her voice.

"They will be out, we will reach someone soon," I reassured her. "Remember, we need to be within two hundred miles of another aircraft and within its line of sight for it to pick up our call, just keep trying every few minutes."

She'd broadcast perhaps a half-dozen times when an ecstatic response crackled back, "Good morning C-ADXH, it's mighty good to hear from you, you've had us real worried. Lots of folks out looking for you, fearing the worst. "What's your location and status?"

I took over the communication. "I have seven persons on-board, two requiring urgent medical assistance upon landing." I tried to keep it formal, wanting to blurt out the whole story but realising that with the airport approaching there would be better times for tale telling. "We are bound for Old Crow, ETA about forty-five minutes. I have damaged landing gear and need guidance on how to land the plane."

"C-ADXH, what kind of damage are we talking about?"

"I have no tail wheel."

"C-ADXH, with no tail wheel you'll have to land on the main gear and keep your nose up, can you manage that?"

"Umm, I'm not sure, I haven't actually flown a plane before, I'm going to need any guidance you can give me to get the plane down."

A pause. "C-ADXH, is this Jim Carter speaking?"

"No, this is Nate Ellis, Jim Carter is incapacitated, I'm flying the plane."

Another pause, "okay Nate, is Mr Carter beside you and able to offer any assistance at all?

"No, he's in a coma, I have Emmi Fallon with me in the cockpit."

"You performed the take-off and are flying solo?!"

"I did, I am."

"Where are you now?"

"We're seventy-five miles due south of Old Cow, flying at ninety-five knots."

"Well, ..., this is not a conversation I expected be having." I could hear the amazement in the man's voice. "Okay look, my name is Jake, and I have co-pilot Alice Duggan up here with me.

"Hi Nate, Emmi, wow, the two of you are really something, you're doing great and you're in the best hands with Jake here," Alice greeted us.

"We took off from Old Crow about twenty minutes ago, we're routed towards Dawson City but I'm coming round now," Jake continued. We'll be with you in about ten minutes, look out for me coming up on your port side. We're going be flying right alongside you, slightly above and behind, we'll escort you all the way to the airfield and talk you safely in.

That sounded so fantastic I wanted to cry. "Maintain your heading and fly slowly at ninety knots until we intercept. You stay on this frequency and talk to me, don't go fiddling with that dial to try to reach the airport in case you get the frequency wrong and we lose communication with you all together. Alice here will use our other radio to speak to the airport. Is there any other damage to the plane?"

"Just bumps and scrapes, nothing that should cause us any problems. I took off with only about seventeen litres of oil though."

"Seventeen litres, right. What's the oil temperature now?"

I checked the dial; the needle was creeping up. "It's at eighty degrees."

"Right, eighty degrees is high but not problematic. Just keep an eye on it, tell me if it changes. Ninety-five degrees is the maximum temperature, go above that and you'll damage the engine. Obviously getting you onto the ground at Old Crow safely is the priority, I don't care what damage you do to the plane in the meantime as long as you don't do it too far out for you to get into that airport."

"Right-oh," I acknowledged, "slowing to ninety

knots now, I'll keep checking the oil temperature." I eased back on the throttle and watched the speed fall on the dial. When it hit ninety knots Emmi gave me a thumbs up, she seemed much cheerier and more relaxed too.

"C-ADXH, how you doing Nate? I'm coming up on you now. I have visual and can confirm your tail wheel is missing." Jake paused communication for a moment.

"Okay, so I assume, since you managed to take off and get this far you know something about flying.

"Jim Carter taught me a lot of theory, I've read tons of books and I've been using Microsoft Flight Simulator for over a year. The Otter has a Pilot Operating Handbook on it, I've studied it and studied it over the last few days."

"Great stuff, you're gonna do just fine. Now, landing on two wheels is a little trickier than landing on three, but it's perfectly possible: Those front wheels are very close to the plane's centre of gravity, you can come down on them without tipping forwards if you do it right. I'm going to talk you through it now, just stop me at any point if you don't understand Son."

"'kay."

"Right, so, what you don't want to do is hit the runway on those front wheels and wheelbarrow off. Approach the runway slightly faster than usual - go for seventy knots but whilst you keep your airspeed up, you'll need to curb your vertical speed to ensure that the touchdown on the main gear is gentle. You'll need to flare - pitch your nose up - five to ten foot above the runway to increase the lift on the wings and cut the rate of descent."

"Jeez," muttered Emmi. "Just words, random, meaningless words!"

I was following though. No book I'd ever read had described the technique Jake was suggesting, I told him it was the first time I'd heard of it. He gave a small snuffle of a laugh. "You'll not find it in any manuals Nate, it's a bad technique, not one people write about, but I give you my word it'll work better than any other method in this situation."

"So, after you flare, your airspeed will wash off – the drag will slow you down. If you give a blip of power - a burst of throttle, one hundred rpm or so - you'll increase your lift and airspeed but cut your vertical speed -your rate of descent and smooth your touchdown. You will use up more runway though, if you think you're going to run out you'll have to power back up and go-round – I'll come back to that in a minute."

"Just after you touchdown, you want to add a little forward stick to reduce the angle of attack and stop the plane bouncing back up. Arc you with me so far?"

I was visualising it all in my mind, surprising myself by remaining calm enough to follow it logically through. I was interested, rather than horrified which was good. What Jake had said so far made sense. After I'd flared the nose would be up, I'd need to push on that control column to keep it down.

"Got it," I said with a reasonable amount of confidence.

"Don't be too reticent about pushing forwards," Jake continued, "it takes quite a bit of force to make the propeller strike the runway."

"Yep," I replied, "been there and done that on take-off, I've got a fair idea of how far I can go."

"Riiight," he replied, I could tell he was dying to hear all about it, but he stuck to the matter in hand. "Now, as I said, I've just come from Old Crow, you need to be aware there's a fair crosswind from the left today which is going to complicate things a bit for you."

'Fantastic – a bit of added complication, just what we needed!!'

"Don't worry too much about it, the runway at Old Crow's is thirty meters wide - not super wide but broad enough to give you a bit of drift room. You'll need to counteract the push of that wind: Point your nose towards the wind, just five or ten degrees off the centre-line. When you're just above the runway and about to land, kick the tail to straighten up by squeezing the right rudder. Dip the left wing into the wind which will bring you down on your left wheel first if you can. Do you understand?"

I processed the manoeuvre in my head, "I do," I said at last. And I did, I got the theory well enough, whether I could put it into practice and land without cartwheeling us into the ground and horrific injury or death was an altogether different matter!

"If you bounce," Jake went on, "let the plane descend again, flare for your landing attitude – get your nose up and increase that angle of attack – then attempt another landing if you have enough runway left. If not, perform a go-round – pitch up, add full power and retract flaps, circle and come back in for another shot."

For the remainder of the journey I ran the landing through my mind over and over, clarifying some aspects with Jake. I was dimly aware of Jake informing Emmi that Alice had made contact with Old Crow. Everyone there was delighted we were alive, they were keeping the runway clear for us coming in and would have emergency services on the airfield just in case. 'Alive for the moment,' I thought ruefully and knew everyone else would be thinking the same thing. I was dreading the airport coming into view, I was doing okay, flying along nicely, we were safe up here. I fought the strong compulsion just to keep going. 'More accidents happen during landing than at any other time during flight,' a voice inside my head reminded me. "Yeah, yeah, but few of them involve fatalities," I replied, "I just need to get us down alive; it doesn't need to be a good landing." Emmi turned to me startled and I realised I'd spoken out loud.

I was about to try to explain but Jake's voice stopped me, "here we go Nate, time to do some work. We're about twenty-five miles out of Old Crow now." I tensed, this was it, could I do it?

"The airport's eight hundred and twenty-four feet above sea level, I want you to descend to three thousand feet on the altimeter, that's roughly two thousand, two hundred feet above the ground. In about five miles I want you to come round to the right, a thirty degree turn onto a heading of 030. Once you've made the turn, lower your flaps to get your speed down, use the landing setting on the flaps lever, Full Flaps is not necessary, you only need that for a very short runway."

The runway at Old Crow was one thousand, four hundred and ninety-four meters long, the Otter, specifically designed for short take-off and landing, only needed four hundred meters to land, full flaps were not required, the landing setting would be sufficient. I reviewed Jake's instructions and nodded. Realised he couldn't see me and confirmed I understood and agreed with his strategy. I was reassured and grateful for his caution, he was preparing me for as easy and relaxed a ride in as possible. Twenty miles out was way early for putting flaps down, but Jake was giving me plenty of time to get myself sorted for landing. The flaps would allow me to fly more slowly without having to keep my nose up to stop me falling from the sky. Keeping my nose down would allow me to see out of the window, get a visual on the airport as soon as possible. At ninety knots I was already below the maximum speed for lowering the flaps and I still had plenty of fuel, there was no reason not to just get it done.

"At seven miles out, we'll begin our descent, your approach speed should be about eighty knots, slowing to seventy knots for the final descent before landing. Stall speed's forty knots on the Otter with flaps out, so at seventy you've got plenty of leeway if your speed washes-off more than it should - you'll be in no danger of dropping to the ground." I did some quick mental calculations and nodded again, agreeing. I'd be descending at a rate of three hundred feet a minute, I'd have a full seven minutes from the top of descent to landing – a good stretch of time, keeping well above the stall speed was a good, safe plan.

"Got it, descend to three thousand feet now, come round to a heading of 030 in five miles, landing flaps out after the turn, slow to about eighty knots. At seven miles out begin my descent at a rate of three hundred feet per minute, final descent at a rate of seventy knots."

"Good Man."

'Remember to roll out of that turn ten degrees before you reach your heading, so you don't overshoot,' I heard Jim's voice in my head. I'd missed the heading when he'd given me control of the Otter before the crash. I needed to get it right this time so that I was coming into the airport on the correct line.

Emmi read through the short descent, approach and final descent checklists and I changed settings as instructed and confirmed checks. When we'd done I eased off on the power and watched the altimeter fall to three thousand feet. Then I turned the control wheel to the right, using a little back pressure and a bit of right rudder, feeling the ailerons roll the plane in a right bank.

I began my roll out ten degrees before I hit the heading and, as we completed the turn, the airport came into view. I was chuffed I'd got the turn right, but the first sight of the airport sent fear coursing through me. I froze momentarily. "Flaps," prompted Emmi, I gave myself a shake and pulled the lever.

"Keep an eye on that speed for me," I said to her. "The drag from the flaps should slow us to eighty knots." I watched the Vertical Speed Indicator, waiting for it to indicate the three hundred feet rate of descent, it showed two hundred. I eased back on the throttle, taking some power off and the VSI quickly dropped to five hundred feet. More power, I see-sawed unprofessionally backwards and forwards for a few minutes until I got it right. Correct heading, three hundred feet rate of descent, eighty knots on the Air

first approach, stay as calm as you can, you'll be fine."

For the next five minutes, I checked and re-checked the dials in sequence: Air Speed Indicator – in the green zone, don't go below seventy knots; Attitude Indicator – wings level; Altimeter – altitude falling steadily; Vertical Speed Indicator – maintaining rate of descent – three hundred feet per minute.

I won't pretend any of it was pretty, we wandered back and forth along our approach line and I had the plane's nose up, then down making rapid pitch adjustments in response to airspeed changes. 'Chasing the Needles,' Jim had called it I remember, said it was a common rookie mistake. Still, we were about right at one thousand feet, I pulled the throttle out part way and reduced our speed further. Twenty feet and the wind had pushed us nicely onto the centre line, things were looking good. The runway was rushing up to meet us, out of the corner of my eye I could see Emmi pushing backwards into her seat, bracing herself for impact.

Bang! We hit the runway hard - smashed into it - and bounced right back up, the plane tilted, tipped and hurtled forwards, eating up the runway fast. Emmi squeaked, then caught herself, there were yelps from the cabin.

"Go-round, go-round," even Jake's calm, all in day's work attitude had slipped a bit.

I threw the thrust levers forwards, applying full power and we surged back into the air well before the end of the runway. I was shaking like a leaf and, I think, whimpering a little. "Nooo," I heard Sasha wail from behind. I felt sick with disappointment too, we'd been down, it could have been all over – so near and yet so far.

I glanced at Emmi, she looked gutted as well, but she said nothing other than, "next time," giving me a wavering smile. I was grateful for her control; sometimes what people didn't say was much more important than what they did.

"Don't worry about it Son," Jake's voice was back to determinedly positive, "there's not a pilot out there who hasn't bounced an airplane. Just go-round and come back in for another shot, take your time, line up right. The airport's closed to anyone else right now, there's absolutely no rush to get on the ground."

None except my nerves weren't going to hold out much longer.

"I think you probably forgot to flare, to pull that nose up."

Of course!! "I did," I felt better now I knew what had gone wrong, determined to get it right next time.

"Okay, so come round, line-up again - you got that bang on - descend and at about five feet pull that nose up, pop a bit of power on at the same time so that your rate of descent doesn't fall away too fast, don't want you falling out the sky."

"Got it." Emmi read through the approach and final descent checklists again as we circled round. We rolled back and forth once more as I struggled to get the nose into the cross wind, then began our final descent. This time I knew it was no good from way out, my speed was right, but I was still too high, I was also drifting, I hadn't done enough to counteract the wind and we were being blown to the right of the runway. I aborted, throttled back up and went round for the second time.

I was dimly aware of Jake advising through the headset, of Emmi running through the checklists again but I blotted them all out. I focused completely, telling myself over and over I could do it, I could do it, bringing the plane round in a wide arc.

My nosing into the wind was more effective this time, the plane canted a little but there was no rolling. At one thousand feet I was a little too fast, but I maintained the descent, flaring a little earlier than Jake had said: At fifteen feet I raised the nose by five degrees and the rate of descent arrested nicely. Getting the nose up early meant we floated a little, using up more runway than was ideal. We touched down on the front wheels and bounced, I pressed forward on the control column, pushing the nose down and the next time we hit the tarmac we stayed there, charging forwards.

In trying to keep the tail, with its missing wheel off the ground, I pushed the nose too hard and the plane pitched forwards, the propeller coming dangerously close to the ground. I yelped and heard Emmi squeal beside me as she instinctively covered her face with her arms, preparing to crash. Miraculously the plane righted itself. 'They're built to stay upright,' Jim had said, 'a fair bit can go wrong before a plane will allow itself to be smashed into the ground nose first. Thank God for that! Desperate for it to be over, I slammed too hard on the brakes and we went into a skid veering off the runway, bumping onto the snow-covered grass. The skis were our salvation, if the wheels had dug in we would have cartwheeled forwards and smashed up for sure. 'Rudder pedals, rudder pedals' my brain screamed, I pushed with my feet and we tipped one way, then the other, Emmi and I lurching back and forth, I continued to brake and finally, we stopped.

Chapter 19

As I turned off the engine, something collapsed inside me. I was dimly aware of the cheers and whoops of the others, of Jake's ecstatic voice over the radio. Could vaguely feel Emmi clapping me on my shoulder but I felt removed from their jubilation. In fact, whatever had held me together during the flight had gone now and suddenly I was, I was appalled to realise, crying. Not steady, attractive movie style crying either but unstoppable blubbering – shuddering and howling with fat tears pouring down my face, mixing with rivers of snot from my nose and dripping off my chin.

The cockpit was now full, everyone piling in on top of each other. Luke grabbed me and pulled me against his chest, though it must have hurt him to do so, then I felt many other arms around me, cheeks pushing against mine, wet against wet. I tried to stand, found I was stuck, I tried again and again. Libby reached across from where she sat in the right-hand seat, on top of Sasha who was on top of Emmi and unclipped my harness. 'Harness, right!' I threw my arms around the girls, felt Luke's one arm around me, Harvey thumping me on the shoulder, so hard Luke wasn't going to be the only one with a broken collar bone. We clung together, a laughing, crying little band, whilst we watched Jake coming into land perfectly and cars and ambulances streaming towards us.

Luke and Jim were whisked into an ambulance but the rest of us waved away medical attention. On jelly legs I wobbled out of the plane to be swept into a huge bear-hug by Jake, a bearded giant of a man, who'd came charging across the grass from his plane.

"You did it, you did it," he hollered over and over.

"Thank you," I managed, before mortifyingly, I burst out crying again, collapsing into his bulk.

A car whisked us from the runway to the little terminal in minutes, Harvey's loud braying voice competing with Sasha's high excited one the entire way, I didn't hear what either said. Their words just swirled around me as I sat, stunned, unable to take anything in.

It felt like a thousand people mobbed us as we

stepped out of the car, surrounding us rugby scrum style, cheering, shaking hands, clapping shoulders, hugging. Whilst the weather had been too bad for anyone to reach our valley it seemed it had been decent enough for half the world to reach Old Crow! Harvey was last out of the car and I saw him take one look at the milling, yelling throng and climb back in, shutting the door firmly behind him. A woman, I assumed to be Mrs Fallon, pushed her way through the crowd and slipped quietly in beside him. Then there they were, right in front of me, Mum and Colin, Mum hauled me to her, and we clung to each other, laughing and crying at the same time. I pulled back finally and stared at Colin in amazement, "you're here? I didn't think you'd ever get on a plane?"

Colin looked at me equally astonished, "are you kidding, for you I'd get on a rocket to the moon! I even paid to park the car at the airport." I grinned at him, I knew it was true, he would do anything for me, he loved me. Loved me in a way my real dad never had or ever would. Colin would never leave me or Mum, would always be there for us. I'd been horrible to him since he'd arrived in our lives and he'd been nothing but devoted to us. I threw my arms around him and Mum hugged us both, we stood there in the midst of all the chaos, a family reunited.

"We're so proud of you Nate," Colin stuttered, his voice breaking. "Thank God you spent all that time with Jim, learned how to fly."

"It was actually the time I spent with you in the garage that allowed me to work out what had gone wrong with the plane so we could fix it. The oil filter had worked lose, if I'd not watched you torqueing one tight I'd never have known it needed to be done. You got us out really." Colin sobbed noisily and hugged me even tighter.

"You should ring your dad," Mum said when we finally drew apart. "He'll be worried."

Not worried enough to be here waiting for me like you guys I thought. I looked at Colin who was still snuffling and wiping his eyes, hanging onto my arm as though he'd never let me go again. "My dad's right here," I smiled at him, blushing – I sounded ridiculously theatrical and mushy - "I'll phone my father when we get back to the hotel."

Luke arrived at the hotel that evening, he hadn't needed surgery. His arm was strapped, and he'd had some kind of an injection for his broken ribs. He was on strong painkillers and looked much better. "Be fine once I can master my game with just my left hand," he said, waggling his re-charged iPad.

Jim had regained consciousness several times during the day and had even smiled at his son and wife before slipping away again - great signs - the doctors thought he'd be okay. We could all visit tomorrow.

The next morning, after a good night's sleep, a long hot bath and an enormous breakfast we gathered in the hotel lobby. It seemed the world had been waiting with baited breath to see if we'd be found alive; that we'd not only survived but, as a bunch of kids, had repaired the plane and flown ourselves back to safety was, it appeared, a huge story, the press was desperate to speak to us. Our parents, after consulting us, had agreed we'd meet them for a very short time.

It stunned me that everyone was still talking about the crash as though it had just happened.

Objectively, I realised it had, we'd gone down only five days ago, but to me it felt like a lifetime had passed since then. We'd gone through so much. My memory of the crash had already faded into a blur of terrifying snippets and tumultuous emotions – scar tissue from the trauma that would probably remain forever, a parasite on my soul. I wasn't sure I'd have much to tell the waiting throng.

The hotel manager opened the conference room door and the noise of the milling, braying journalists hit us. "Too much," Harvey howled, clapping his hands on his ears and turning tail.

"Too much all right," I agreed. I surveyed the room with trepidation. "Tell you what, I'll go in for fifteen minutes then meet you out on the terrace – how does that sound?"

"The quiet one right around the back?"

"The quiet one right around the back, see you soon buddy."

The rest of us were herded forwards. "Hi, I'm Luke Fallon," said Luke, stepping into the room ahead of me and offering his left hand to a waiting journalist.

"And I'm Lu…., I'm Nate," I said, pushing back my shoulders and diving into the ocean of self-belief. "Nate Ellis."

There are some great organisations out there if you are a young person with an interest in aviation and some fantastic air shows and museums to visit. Here is a list of some of them:

Organisation	WebAddress
Red Bull Air Racing	airrace.redbull.com
Air Shows – UK	
Abingdon Air & Country Show	abingdonairandcountry.co.uk
Air show London	airshowlondon.com
Battle of Britain Air show	bobairshow.co.uk
British Air shows (Airshows Calender)	britishairshows.com
Clacton Air show	clactonairshow.com
Dunsfold Wings & Wheels	wingsandwheels.net
Eastbourne Airborne Air show	eastbourneairshow.com
RAF Cosford Air show	cosfordairshow.co.uk
Sunderland Air show	sunderlandinternationalairshow.co.uk
The Royal International Air Tattoo	airtattoo.com
Aviation Museums - UK	
Avro Museum	avroheritagemuseum.co.uk
Brooklands Museum	brooklandsmuseum.com
Duxford Air Museum	iwm.org.uk
RAF Museum	rafmuseum.org.uk
Stow Maries Great War Aerodrome	stowmaries.org.uk
Vintage Aviation Museum	vintageaviationmuseum.com
Flying Clubs - UK	
Clacton Aero Club	clactonaeroclub.co.uk
Aviation Organisations - UK	

Air League	airleague.co.uk
Air Scouts	members.scouts.org.uk/supportresources/188/air-scouting-introduction
Aircraft Owners & Pilots Association	aopa.org
Aviation Skills Partnership	aviationskillspartnership.com
British Air Displays Association	bada-uk.com
British Gliding Association	gliding.co.uk
British Model Flying Association	bmfa.org
Brownies & Guides Aviation Studies	girlguiding.org.uk
Classic Wings	classic-wings.co.uk
RAF Air Cadets	raf.mod.uk/aircadets
Royal Aeronautical Society	aerosociety.com
Royal Institute of Navigation	rin.org.uk
The Light Aircraft Association	lightaircraftassociation.co.uk
Air Shows - US	
Abbotsford International Air show	abbotsfordairshow.com
California Capital Air Show	californiacapitalairshow.com
California Capital Air Show	californiacapitalairshow.com
Chennault International Air show	chennaultairshow.com
Dayton Air Show	daytonairshow.com
Duluth Air Show	duluthairshow.com
Flying Circus Air Show	FlyingCircusAirshow.com
Fort Wayne Air show	fwairshow.com/
Greenwood Lake Air Show	greenwoodlakeairshow.com
HAPO Air Show	waterfollies.com
Montrose County Tribute to Aviation	tributetoaviation.com
New Smyma Balloon & Sky Fest	newsmymabeachballoonandskyfest.com
Peace Regional Air show	peaceregionalairshow.com
Southern Most Air Spectacular	airshowkeywest.com
Stuart Air show	stuartairshow.com
Tribute to Aviation	tributetoaviation.com

Truckee Tahoe Air Show	TruckeeTahoeAirshow.com
Aviation Organisations - US	
AOPA (Aircraft Owners & Pilots Association)	aopa.org
Florida Institute of Technology	floridatech.edu.
Ninety Nines	ninety-nines.org
Sun & Fun Fly In	flysnf.org
Flying Clubs – US	
Aero sport Ltd	flyaerosport.com
Harris Hill Soaring Corporation	harrishillsoaring.org
Mast Cove Seaplane Base	MastCoveSeaplane.com
Waterloo Warbirds	waterloowarbirds.com
Aviation Museums - US	
99s Museum of Women Pilots	museumofwomenpilots.org
Air Zoo	airzoo.org
Amelia Earhart Birthplace Museum	ameliaearhartmuseum.org
Castle Air Museum	castleairmuseum.org
Cavanaugh Flight Museum	cavflight.org
Cincinnati Aviation Museum	cahslunken.org
Commemorative Air Force	commemorativeairforce.org
Golden Age Air Museum	goldenageair.com
Historic Aircraft Squadron Museum	historicalaircraftsquadron.com
National Aviation Hall of Fame	nationalaviation.org
National Soaring Museum	soaringmuseum.org
National Warplane Museum	nationalwarplanemuseum.org
Rhinebeck Aerodrome Museum	oldrhinebeck.org
Strategic Air Command & Aerospace Museum	SACMuseum.org
Tomorrows Aeronautical Museum	tamuseum.org

Waco Air Museum	wacoairmuseum.org
Wright Museum	wwbirthplace.com
Yankee Air Museum	yankeeairmuseum.org
Aviation Summer Camps - US	
Aviation Summer Camp Connecticut	aerospaceadventurers.com
Embry Riddle Aeronautical University Summer Camp	summercamps.erau.edu
Florida Institute of Technology	floridatech.edu.
Illinois Aviation Academy	Illionoisaviation.com
Minnesota Aviation Career Education Camp	mnacecamp.org
Western Michigan college of Aviation	wmich.edu/aviation/future/aviationsummercamp
Flying Clubs - Canada	
Abbotsford Flying Club	abbotsfordflyingclub.ca
Aerosport Ltd	flyaerosport.com
Brampton Flying Club	bramptonflightcentre.com
Kamloops	kamloopsflyingclub.com
Kelowna	kelownaflyingclub.com kelownaflyingclub.com/copa-for-kids
MH Aviation	mhaviation.com
Pacific Flying Club	pacificflying.com
Stanley Sport Aviation	stanleysportaviation.ns.ca
Air shows - Canada	
Abbotsford Air Show	abbotsfordairshow.com
Atlantic Canada International Air show	airshowatlantic.ca
Aviation Museums - Canada	
Alaska Aviation Museum	alaskaairmuseum.org
Alberta Aviation Museum	albertaaviationmuseum.org
Atlantic Canada Aviation Museum	acamuseum.ca

British Columbia Aviation Museum	bcam.net
Canada Aviation and Space Museum	ingeniumcanada.org/casm
Canadian Museum of Flight	canadianflight.org
Canadian Warplane Heritage Museum	warplane.com
Greenwood Military Aviation Museum	gmam.ca/flightline-cafe.html
Illinois Aviation Museum	illinoisaviationmuseum.org
Jet Aircraft Museum	jetaircraftmuseum.ca/
National Air Force Museum of Canada	airforcemuseum.ca
The Great War Flying Museum	greatwarflyingmuseum.org
Vintage Wings of Canada	vintagewings.ca
Other – Canada	
Air Zoo	airzoo.org
Alaska Airmen Association	alaskaairmen.org
COPA for Kids	copanational.org/en/copa-for-kids
Elevate Aviation	elevateaviation.ca
Mast Cove Seaplane	mastcoveseaplane.com
Women in Aerospace Canada	wia-canada.org

Author's website

www.jetimlin.com